Blood of the Curse

Blood of the Curse

by D.C. Cole

Editor
Kurt Conrad

Senior Publisher
Steven Lawrence Hill Sr.

Awarded Publishing House
ASA Publishing Company

ASA Publishing Company
Nominated For 2012,2013 BBB Torch Award
105 E. Front St., Suite. 101, Monroe, Michigan 48161
www.asapublishingcompany.com

Copyrights©2013 D.C. Cole, All Rights Reserved
Book: Blood of the Curse
Date Published: 01.07.2014
Edition: 1 *Trade Paperback*
Book ASAPCID: 2380617
ISBN: 978-1-886528-62-8
Library of Congress Cataloging-in-Publication Data

This book was published in the United States of America.
State of Michigan

A Publisher Trademark Title page

Blood of the Curse

This book is a story about four friends, all women who go on an excursion to get away from the hustle and bustle of city life. Unbeknownst to them they are the victims of witchcraft. Two witches use an old family legend and family history to prey upon their fears and weaknesses to gain access to a family fortune. The witches' plan backfires due to an accident and powers given to one of the women.

Table of Contents

Blood of the Curse

by D.C. Cole

CHAPTER 1

On the Road Again,...

As we gathered our bags and loaded them into the jeep, we couldn't control our excitement; we were finally going on our girl's weekend. The mountain was calling our name. Skiing, dining, sitting around the fireplace sipping wine; it sounds wonderful. It has been so long since we had all gotten together; no husbands, no boyfriends, no kids, and no one asking where are my socks, have you seen my briefcase, and no worries etc., just a relaxing time with the girls.

"Hey Natasha, what are you doing?" Ivy called from the passenger seat. It had been months since we had seen each other, we had always been great friends, and we were college roommates. She just got married to this guy who seems like Mr. Perfect, but I think he is hiding something. "Seriously Natasha lets go, kiss your hubby and move it," Ivy hollered at me.

"Ok," I said, as I went to my husband who was standing there with my son, waiting to kiss me good bye. "I love you sweetie," I said as I kissed Seth good bye, *Man, I love that man*, I thought. *He is truly amazing*. "Good bye little man," I said to my son. He is only four, but he is such a big boy, "Now you be good for Seth, and listen to him. I will call and say good night to you tonight," I warned him. He was a good boy, just full of fire, "I love you guys," I called as I went to the jeep. I have never spent a night away from Seth, and I have never been away from Jack, my little man, except when I am work, but I know he is in good hands. I looked back one more time, before I got in, this is going to be difficult, but it is going to be a great weekend.

"Sammy, how have you been?" Ivy asked as we pulled out of the driveway. I hadn't seen her in a long time. She worked at an advertising firm and was making a pretty decent living. She was always pushing herself to be the best. I have never seen her with a steady boyfriend; it was always all work and no play.

"Oh I have been great, I just got promoted to Creative Director at the firm, so now I get my own assistant and a big raise, she boasted. I love my boss. He is always very calm, and never yells at people," Sammy said.

That is awesome, Trish said. Sammy and Trish were also college roommates, and Trish and I have been friend since we were children. We all came together through each other, and all three of them stood up for me at my wedding to Seth. They were the three best friends a girl could ask for.

"So girls are you ready for a stress free weekend?" Ivy asked us. Yes, we all said at once. "Hey Natasha, may I please see that crack berry of yours?" Ivy asked. Those phones are as addicting as crack. "No seriously, Natasha. Toss me your phone," Ivy said with an eerie laugh.

"Yes, but it is a blackberry," I said correcting her slam against my cell phone. I wasn't sure why she wanted my phone, with her you can never be too sure. She was always up to something. She has always been the one who loved games, and messing with people.

"Oh, no it's a crack berry," she laughed as I handed her my phone. "Thank you. Now you are only allowed to use this to call and say good night to your son. I will keep it safe for you," she taunted me. "I know you probable have some dead line or something, but this weekend is our weekend, and there is no work, or stress allowed," Ivy taunted me.

"No. Please give it back. I am expecting an email from my publisher. Please?" I begged. "I didn't tell him I was unavailable this weekend," I said hoping she would give in. "Ivy, please," I begged.

"I will give it back if you promise to not use your laptop all weekend," she bargained. "You can email from your phone or your computer, so pick one," she said. "Besides, either way you are only going to send one email and that is to say, you will be back on Tuesday," she said giggling uncontrollably at my defeat.

"Ok, keep my phone," I said giving in. She knew full well I couldn't stay off my laptop. "I am in the middle of a new contract with my publisher." "I need to be able to email him the final draft of my novel," I said hoping they would understand. "You win. But I do need it to say good night to Seth and Jack," I said sternly.

"I promise I will give it back to you, so you can say good night to the family. I would never be that cruel," Ivy said sincerely. "Besides, I know you have never gone away without either of them and you haven't spent a night away from Seth since you met," she teased. "I promise everything will be ok, and you will enjoy this new thing called a vacation," she teased.

"So Ivy, how is married life treating you?" I asked trying to change the subject. She just got married a month or so ago, and it was completely out of the blue. None of us knew she was even seeing anyone, let alone getting married, until she came back from a so called business trip, married.

"Oh, it's great. Lance is a dream. All he wants to do is be with me and take care of me. He is perfect," she said with a sigh. "Every morning he goes to the coffee shop and gets me my morning caramel macchiato and blueberry scones," she said with a sigh of happiness. "When we go out to dinner with his bosses or clients, he refers to me as his queen. His bosses love it when I come, because they say family is important to their clients, and a man that treats his wife the way he treats me will treat their clients just as good," she said with a giggle. "Did you see our picture in the paper?" Ivy asked, handing me the paper.

"Why was your picture in the paper?" I asked as I opened the paper. "That is a really good picture of you two. Your hair looks amazing," I said handing the paper to Trish. I couldn't help but wonder what he had up his sleeve; no one can be that perfect. I was glad that she regarded him as wonderful and treated her well, but I got the feeling that he was hiding something. I just couldn't figure it out. I hadn't told her what I thought, only because I didn't want to hurt her. She was really happy and I didn't want to be skeptical if there was no reason to, but the first time he did something to hurt her, I would find out.

"It is going to be long drive girls, so we better pop the cork on that bottle wine," Trish said. "It will make the trip a little more fun, and not seem so long," Trish offered, as if she had to twist our arm. "Ivy, you do look amazing, and Lance is pretty cute too," she said skimming through the paper. Hey guys, did you see the story on the front page, she said looking at it closely. "Hey guys, I think this is where we are going," she said as we scooted closer to her.

"It is where we are going. It says 'four young women were the victims of mother nature's wrath', Trish read. 'A sporadic vengeful avalanche hit the mountains and took the lives of a young author...' Trish stopped in mid-sentence and said, "You guys this is us," she said stunned by what she was seeing.

"It can't be; we haven't even been to the slopes yet," Ivy said. "Give me that," she said and snatched the paper out of Trish's hands. "Oh my goodness, it is us, but how?" she cried.

"Ok, guys this is obviously a joke," Sammy said calmly. "We are alive, and kicking," she said laughing. "Come on, let's not get worked up. We know it isn't real, so take a drink of your wine, and relax," Sammy said.

"Ok, I guess she is right," I said still alarmed by the sight of that, but it had to be just a stupid joke. Hey pass the bottle, I said. "Forget about the paper and throw it out the window. I am not going to let a dumb joke ruin our weekend," I said taking a drink.

"Ok, but I am not going to drink, I will drive," Sammy said. She has always been the safe girl who never does anything wrong "Drinking and driving is very dangerous. I want to enjoy our weekend and not come home in a body cast or bag," she said in a very stern tone.

"Oh come on Sammy, just one drink," Ivy teased. "One drink won't kill you," Ivy taunted her. "Sammy don't you ever do anything wrong, or break any rules?" Ivy asked sarcastically.

"Ok, Ivy leave her alone. She's a good girl; and besides, I would like to enjoy our weekend too," Trish said sticking up for her. "You know Sammy doesn't drink much, and if she feels more comfortable driving sober, then let her," Trish ordered.

Ivy has always been a bit of diva, and loved drama. Trish has always been the loyal one who keeps the piece, and helps keep Ivy grounded. Sammy is the secure one; she doesn't break the rules, and lives her life on a schedule, grounded to her work. I have always been the one that doesn't follow orders. I do my thing, and live my life, that's how I started writing books. I decided one morning that I would write a romance novel, and now I have two romance novels, four children's books, a couple of thrillers out and I am working on another one.

"So Natasha, what is your new book about anyways?" Trish asked me as she handed me the bottle of wine. Trish has been my biggest supporter, and number one fan, since the very first book. She teases me all the time, about being my stalker, and getting bobble heads made of me. She has always been there for me no matter what. "I know you always tell me you can't say until it's done, but one of these days you will crack and give us a sneak peak," Trish teased.

"You know I can't tell you yet. It's got to be a surprise," I said laughing, because I do always tell her that. One of these days I might give her a sneak peak, maybe.

"So, how much further till the lodge?" I asked. It seemed we had all forgotten about the paper, and were ready to have a good night. I couldn't wait to get there; room service, soft comfy pillows, the works, I thought. This weekend was long overdue. I really needed it, more than I could describe. Seth is always telling me, I need to take time out for myself, and relax, but until now I haven't listened. He is wonderful. He told the girls I was in before I even knew about it, and set everything up for me to go. How I love that man. He is wonderful.

"Well, we are about half way there, so probably another two hours to go," Sammy said. "Does anyone have any water or coffee?" Sammy asked.

"Yeah, I brought some water, and of course we all know I have coffee," I said to her laughing. "Everyone knows I have coffee, it is my life line. Seth always teases me about putting coffee in an IV drip. Do you need cream or anything for the coffee?" I asked.

"No, I can drink it black. I just feel like coffee is missing from hand right now," she said laughing as she took the coffee I handed her. She took a sip, "Wow Natasha do you always make your coffee so strong?" Sammy asked with a laugh.

"Sorry, I like strong coffee; I love the flavor of it," I said." I have this coffee at home. Its Dunkin Donuts brand, and its Dunkin Turbo. It is the perfect wake up call, especially when you know you have a lot to do in the morning," I said bragging about my coffee selection.

"Natasha I swear, you are a freak with your coffee addiction," Ivy said laughing. "You are the only girl I know that packs coffee before wine on a girl's weekend getaway," she teased. She was right though, I did love my coffee, sometimes too much.

"Hey Sammy, take the next right on that dirt road, its short cut," Ivy said. "We used to take this road all the time, when we would come up here," Ivy said trying to convince Sammy to turn there.

"I don't know Ivy. I don't like your short cuts. They normally get us lost," Sammy said. "Besides Ivy, you haven't been up here in years. Are you sure it's even drivable still?" Sammy asked skeptically. Sammy was right. Ivy hadn't been here in a long time and she was always trying to take short cuts, and stuff. Because her parents were very well off, she's been taking the easy way her whole life. Her parents were the reason we afford this weekend. They are shareholders at the lodge, so we didn't have to pay a dime for this weekend.

"Ok, I'll take it," Sammy said reluctantly and turned down the dirt road. "I'm warning you Ivy, if this gets us lost, I am going to slap you upside your head, and hope it knocks some direction into you," Sammy said laughing. It wasn't very often that Sammy cracked a joke, or threatened anyone, but Ivy can make her that way.

"So Trish, what has been going on with you?" I asked, noticing she had been somewhat quiet this trip, and trying to keep Sammy and Ivy from getting into a scuffle. "You've been awfully quiet. Are you alright?" I asked, hoping she was ok.

"Well, I started seeing this really amazing guy. He has a good job and two kids as well. The kids and I get along great, and we're getting married this spring," she said holding up her hand with a huge rock on it. "I was going to wait to tell you at the lodge," Trish said trying to keep the tears of joy away.

"Oh my goodness. That's amazing! Congratulations! When did it happen?" I asked trying to control my excitement. "I didn't even know you were seeing anyone. Why is that?" I asked. My mind was racing. I had so many questions.

"Well, it just kind of happened. We've only been seeing each other for about six months, but it just feels so right," she said hoping we wouldn't get judgmental. "I know it seems rushed, but he is amazing. He makes me feel like a princess, and I love him," she said.

"Hey when you know, you just know. I was only with Seth a month and a half before I asked him to marry me," I said hoping she would feel better. "I'm so happy for you Trish," I said.

"You know Natasha you are a freak! You eat like a pig and never gain pound. One day, right out of the blue, you decide to start writing romance novels, and you're actually good at it," Ivy said. "You tell us you are never getting married and you don't need a man, and the next thing you know you asked Seth to marry you and you're planning a wedding," Ivy said laughing so hard she had a tear in her eye.

"Oh, you're just too funny Ivy," I said laughing. She was right, I never did anything the normal way, and if I got a bug up my butt and decided to do something, I'd do it. "Okay, let's be nice," I said threatening her.

"Trish, I am so happy for you," I said, grabbing the bottle of wine and toasting to her and her future. We laughed and toasted to Trish, and then offered the bottle to Sammy. I only offered because I didn't want her to feel left out. I didn't try to force it on her.

"I would love to toast to Trish," Sammy said taking the bottle from hand. We were stunned and silent. "I know what you are all thinking, but this is an exception to the rule. It's for Trish, and I am so happy she found her happy ending. I am happy we all have found our happy endings," she said as she took a fairly big drink from the bottle.

"Sammy, thank you," Trish said still stunned by her words and reaction. "It means a lot to me that you are willing to join the celebration right now," she continued. "Yes, to everyone's happy ending," Trish said taking a drink to the toast.

ASA Publishing Company

CHAPTER 2

Dead End

"Ivy, this road is getting bad. Are you sure it is safe?" Sammy asked. "It's turning into a blizzard out here. I thought the weather report said clear skies, and above freezing weather."

"Yeah, it's fine," Ivy said as we drove further down the road. The snow began to fall heavily, and it was turning into a complete white out. We couldn't see two feet in front of us. "It is getting worse out," Ivy said. "The weather report still says clear skies, no snow or anything," Ivy said holding up my phone with the weather report. "Well, our weather man needs to be fired if he can't see it's a blizzard outside," Ivy said annoyed.

"Ok, Ivy I can't see anything but white. Is there a turn ahead or something?" Sammy asked. You could hear the fear in her voice. She was petrified of blizzards. Her parents were killed in a car accident during a blizzard when she was about ten years old and she witnessed the whole thing. She got thrown from the car and was lucky to survive. "Ivy, talk to me please. You know I don't like bad roads, especially when I don't know where I am going," Sammy cried, trying to hold back her tears.

"Hey Sammy I see a cottage up ahead. Pull in there and we will wait until it clears up a bit," I said knowing she was ready to fall apart. I couldn't bear to see Sammy so upset. I couldn't imagine how she felt, I thought.

As we pulled up to the cottage, it was huge. It was like a mansion, but no one was home. "Hey I know this place," Ivy said. "It's my great grandfather's place. I remember coming here when I was a child. He died many years ago, but I bet the key is still under the rug," she said as she got out and went to look. Sure enough, there was a key. "Come on guys, lets grab our bags, and we will just stay the night here," she said.

"Ivy, are you sure?" I asked. "It looks like no one has been here in years," I said skeptically. The sight of this place was strange. I got a very different vibe from it. It was like someone or something was watching us. "Ivy, I don't know about this; it looks dangerous, are you sure it's vacant?" I asked still very unsure about this.

"Yes, I am positive," Ivy said confidently. "My parents hired a man to look after it years ago, she said. They even have him restock the cupboards and bar just in case they need it, and they have him throw out all the expired goods. So, I am totally sure this place is good," she said cockily.

"Natasha, I'm sorry I got scared," Sammy said as we were getting out of the car. I could see the gratefulness in her eyes, she was so happy to be off the road.

"It's alright honey, we all have fears, and I completely understand yours," I said rubbing her arm. "Come on. Let's get inside before we get frost bit, and start our weekend right now. It's Thursday evening, and we don't have to be home until Monday afternoon, so relax," I said trying to make her feel better.

"You're right. Let's start our weekend," she said with a soft smile. "Is there any more of that wine? I could really use a glass or bottle, which ever," Sammy said giggling. I smiled and finished grabbing our bags.

"Natasha, can you believe this place?" Trish came running to me saying. "It's amazing. Everything looks as if it is from the medieval times, all Victorian. If this house could talk, I wonder what it would say," Trish said. She was always into history, and loved taking pictures. "Maybe we should just stay here all weekend," Trish said, full of excitement and curiosity.

"Trish, what are you going to take a picture of first?" I asked, knowing she was dying to start taking pictures.

"You know me to well, Natasha," Trish said as she grabbed her camera, and snapped a picture of me quickly because she knew I hated my picture taken. "I'll get you for that," I said laughing. She knew I hated my picture taken, but yet she still loved to snap quick shots of me when I wasn't looking.

"Hey, what are you guys doing, there is a full bar, and loads of junk food, so what are you waiting for?" Ivy burst in and said. "Come on, let's start this weekend off right now," she said laughing and heading back to living room, where the bar was at.

"Give me one second. I need to call and say good night to my son. Then, I'm hitting that bar," I said with a laugh. "Oh where is my phone? I can't find it anywhere," I asked. I had completely forgotten that Ivy had snatched it from me earlier.

"You might need this," she said handing me my phone." I told you, you are only allowed to call your family, so please just call, and then put it away," she said. "I know you have deadlines, but I really want this weekend to be work free," she said with a sad little puppy dog face.

"Oh yes, I will need that," I said snatching my phone from her hand before she could change her mind, "and I promise to make it a quick call," I said reassuring her of my dedication to the stress free, work free weekend.

"Sammy, I'll pour you a drink while you go change. What's your poison my dear?" she asked in a wicked tone and giggle.

"Ooh, I think I will have some red wine," Sammy said. She knew Ivy was going to give her hell about drinking wine, when we had a full supple of liquor at our disposal.

"Oh living on the edge. You need to step out of your shell every now and then. Come on you are with us. What's it going to hurt if you live a little?" Ivy teased.

"Ok, fine, make me whatever you are drinking," Sammy challenged. Sammy was a bit competitive, especially with Ivy. They always seem to get into an argument whenever we're all together.

"Now you're talking," Ivy snapped. "Are you sure you can handle it?" Ivy asked. She was trying to push Sammy's buttons. "I mean, after all, you are playing with the big dogs now," Ivy taunted her.

"Now you two promise to be nice," I said. I know the two of you thrive on your little competeveness, but this is a fun weekend, and there is no fighting or drama," I warned. They were best friends, but yet they loved the fight. It always amazed me, how they acted; they hated to love each other, but loved hating each other.

"You two are just too funny," I said with a laugh. "Oh go make us some drinks, Ivy, and Sammy go change, and find Trish while you're at it," I ordered.

"I will see you guys in there," I yelled as I went to call my hubby, and baby boy. I looked down at my phone, and I noticed it was a very weak signal to send a text message. *Well, maybe I have enough signal for call*, I thought as I dialed the number. *Damn it! Dropped the call. Ok, I'll text him, and hope he gets 'I love you both very much. I have no service, but I will*

call as soon as I find a phone. Give Jack a hug for me, and tell
him mommy loves him very much, xoxoxo. My cell phone just
keeps saying sending... Ah, finally it sent. Oh wow, he replied
back fast. I opened the message; oh it's not from him, Oh my
goodness, I cried and went running to find the girls.

Ivy is this from you, I screamed at her showing her the
message. Look, I screamed is this some kind of sick joke I
screamed at her. She loved to play games with us, but this was
just sick, and cruel.

"Wow, what are you talking she said looking at my
phone. No, Natasha I didn't send that to you," she said. I could
see by the look in her eyes, she was telling me the truth. "I
swear Natasha, I wouldn't do something that mean. I love
jokes, and pranks, but I would never be this twisted," she said.

"You guys, what does it say?" Trish asked scared to
know the truth. She wasn't much into fiction, and scary
movies. She loved the natural way of things. If anything
seemed a little out there she was the first to run and hide
under a blanket. "Oh my goodness," she cried as she read the
message. I could see in her eyes she was ready to run. "Who's
it from?" she asked quietly.

"It says private number, and there is no way to find
out," I said. That is why I immediately came to Ivy, the
prankster of us all, I said with a very agitated tone in my voice.

"Look guys, it's probably my stupid dim witted
husband," Ivy said trying to make everyone calm down. He is
probably trying to make me scared so I come home. He
wanted me to go away with you guys, but he misses me when
I am gone to the bathroom," she said. It was working a little to
make us a bit more relaxed, but it just made me not trust him
even more.

"Ok, who's ready to have fun?" Sammy came in and
asked "Whoa, who died?" she asked with a laugh. "You all look

like someone just killed your best friend," she said with a laugh.

"That's not funny," I said. "How could you joke about something like that," I snapped at her. I didn't mean to be mean, but I was a little on edge.

"I am sorry. I just meant," she started to say.

"I know but there is a situation," I interrupted. "You have no idea what is happening and I am sorry I snapped at you," I said feeling bad for getting upset with her.

"What's wrong?" she asked, the fear bleeding from her eyes. I showed her the message. "Oh my goodness. We're all going to die," she screamed. She was just as bad as Trish when it came to dramatics.

"Stop it Sammy. We don't need your dramatics right now," Ivy said. "It's probably my husband being a jerk, so let's relax," she said.

"Yeah, you're right," I said. "We need to just have a drink and some fun," I said agreeing with her. *It doesn't surprise me that her husband would do that, just to mess with us. He was a lot like her in that aspect*, I thought. "Ok, guys, we came here to have fun. The message is nothing. Let's just ignore it. It's probably Ivy's husband," I said, holding my tongue on what I really wanted to call him.

"Ok, let's toast," Trish said handing us each a shot. "A toast to our weekend of fun," she said holding up her shot glass.

"What is this?" I asked scared to know what she gave us. I smelled it, "Its tequila," I said shocked by Trish's choice.

"Oh, I can't drink this you guys. You know what happens, when I drink tequila," Sammy said blushing. "Come on guys, you remember me with tequila. I get too drunk and silly," she said trying not to say what she really does.

"Oh yes we do Sammy. But, who cares? You are here with us. There aren't any random guys for you to make out with," I said handing her a shot, and calling her out on her make out sessions with random guys.

"Fine," she said taking the shot from my hand. "It's still not nice to call me out like that," she said as her face turned a bright shade of crimson.

"A toast to all of us, our successes, our families and the four best friends any one could ask for," I said holding my glass up, and with the clink of our glasses, and a flip in the wrist, and we felt the burn of the tequila.

"Another message," I gasped. "Oh, it's from my husband," I said, relieved to hear from him. It read, 'I love you too babes. Have fun. I promise I will kiss the little man and tell him you love him. Oh, don't bother using your laptop. I took your battery out, and the charger. I already called the publisher and told him you're away until Tuesday, so relax and enjoy your weekend.' Xoxoxo

"Aw, now isn't that a perfect husband," Trish said sincerely. She was right, he was perfect, I thought. "I hope my marriage is as happy as yours," Trish said sweetly. "Another shot girls," Trish said handing us each another shot of Tequila.

"To Natasha and her success as author, as well as landing the world's most perfect guy."

"Hey what happened to our sipping wine around the fire place?" I asked, as we took our shots again, again and again. We were all feeling kind of tipsy. There was no more burn from it and it was going down way too smooth.

"Ok guys, I need to pass out," Sammy said as she got up, and then fell back down giggling. She was not a drinker, but when she pretended to be it was hysterical.

"Ok, I will take her to bed," I said getting up, and helping her. I could always handle my tequila better than the rest. It was my drink of choice, I thought with a smile. "Now Sammy, don't get friendly with me, you hear?" I said giggling, knowing she likes to kiss when she drinks tequila.

"Ok, Sammy we are going up stairs, so here we go," I said helping her up the stairs. "Natasha, I love you, you are always the level headed one, always so in control," she said as I practically carried her up the stairs.

"Here we are honey, do you need help getting into your pjs?" I asked more as joke.

"Actually yeah, if you don't mind," she said. I was a bit shocked that she wanted help.

She was the one who wrapped up in a towel before she stepped foot out of the shower.

"Ok, where are they at?" I asked. She pointed to the bag on top of the big one. "Sammy, raise your arms," I said as I slipped her shirt over her head. She stood up, and slid her pants down. "Wait a second Sammy, I need to get your shirt on," I said to her, as she stood there totally exposed wearing only her panties. "Sammy, do you need a bucket in case you throw up?" I asked remembering a time when she passed out with her head in a bucket. That was too funny.

"No, I'll be ok; I'm just going to go to sleep now," she said as she lay down on the bed. "I am good," she said as she closed her eyes, and was out.

As I walked down the stairs, I couldn't help but wonder why Sammy was acting that way, she was never so loose and care free. She never does that.

"Hey, she returns," Trish said as I entered the room. "Ivy decided she should pass out too. So, it's you and I sista," she said with a laugh handing me another shot of tequila.

"Wow, so we can hang longer than Ivy," I said with laugh. I felt like I was in high school again. "Sammy, is all tucked in bed and passed out," I said.

"She can't handle her tequila. She never could. It's kind of funny; the only time you see her let loose at all is when she is drunk on tequila," Trish said laughing.

"So Trish, tell me more about this man you are going to marry?" I asked. I was dying to know about her Mr. Perfect.

"He is so sweet. He calls me every morning to say 'Good Morning Beautiful', and every day after work he meets me at the house just to tell me he hopes I had a good day. I have never had any man care so much about me, and make me feel like a princess," she said. "He's a doctor. He works at the hospital. That's how we met. Connor was sick one night, and I had to bring him to the emergency room. It was love at first sight," she said. As I sat there listening to her tell me about him, it seemed so nice to see her happy, she had been hurt so many times, she deserved to be happy. "Yeah, I can't believe things are so well, we decided to wait to move in together, until after we get married," she said.

"That is awesome. It's like a fairy tale or something for you, I am so happy for you," I said. "I couldn't be happier for you. You deserve the best and I hope you get it," I said hugging her.

"Did you hear that?" Trish asked. "What was that?" she asked.

"Another message," I blurted out with terror in my voice. I felt my stomach drop. "I really hope its Seth," I said trying to think positive.

"Open it," Trish demanded.

"It is from a private number again. I don't want to open it," I said.

"Just do it," she ordered out of fear of not knowing what the message said.

'One down three to go. Hahahah, you will never know until it's too late,' I read the message out loud. "What does that mean?" I asked out loud.

"Sammy, Ivy," Trish screamed. "Come on, we have to check on them," she cried.

"You go to Ivy and I will check Sammy," I said, trying to have a plan and make sure they were both ok.

"No, we stay together," she demanded. "If we split up, then who knows what is going to happen," Trish said.

"Ok, come on, I said as we rushed up the stairs." "Sammy," I screamed as we reached the top of the stairs.

"What is going on?" Ivy asked as she came running out? "People are trying to sleep you know, and running around screaming doesn't help," Ivy snapped. She never was one who liked to get woken up.

"We got another message," I cried as I showed her the message, hoping she would drop her crappy attitude when she read it.

"What does that mean?" Ivy asked as she read it? "Are you guys alright?" Ivy asked, realizing it probably wasn't her moronic husband.

"We don't know, but we wanted to check on you two," Trish said. "Yes we are fine," Trish said.

"Well I am fine," Ivy said. "Sammy," Ivy cried. "Oh no! What if she's not?" Ivy screamed dramatically.

"Hey what is going on?" Sammy asked as she came out of her room still wearing only her underwear. I couldn't help but chuckle a little when I saw her.

"You are ok. Thank goodness," I cried as I hugged her. "There is something going on here. If we are all fine, then what did that message mean?" I asked "Why would someone do this; make us think-oh, I can't even finish that sentence," I said.

"Yeah, I am fine," Sammy said. "I am sorry if I scared you, I didn't mean to," she said. "Why is someone being so cruel to us? We never come up here, so it can't be something we did," Sammy said shyly.

"Let's just get down stairs, and go home," Trish said. She was ready to get out of here, and I didn't blame her I was to this place was freaking me right out. "If we leave now, then hopefully we will make it home alive," Trish continued.

I could hear all our heartbeats, beating fast, thump, thump, thump. We were all so afraid to breathe as we walked down stairs. "What about our bags?" Ivy asked. Of course she would be the one to ask that?

"We don't need them, Trish snapped as we reached the door. It's locked!" she gasped.

"Unlock it!" I demanded. "It isn't that hard to unlock a door," I snapped. "I am sorry. I didn't mean to snap, but I am a little freaked out right now," I said hoping she didn't take any offense.

"It won't-there's no lock on it, we can't open it," Trish cried. "How can it be locked without a lock," Trish cried. "Something really weird is going on here you guys," she cried.

"Ok, relax let's just go to the side door, or a window," Ivy said confidently. I wanted to slap her … she always had to be the one who acts better than the rest. "The side door is old and weak, if it's locked we can ram it, and it will open," Ivy said.

"Ok, the side door," Sammy cried. "Come on you guys, I want to get out of here, I don't like horror movies and I feel like we are in one right now," Sammy cried as she ran to side door.

It was locked to, Trish rammed it, and it didn't budge. What do we do, Trish asked? I could hear the panic in her voice.

"Ok, let's go back to living room, and think," I said trying to remain calm. *There has to be something we are missing, but what? Why are there so much unexplained questions*, I thought to myself as we walked cautiously back to the living room.

"Trish, this all seems so weird. We get stuck in a freak snow storm, then we start getting random threats, sent to

Natasha's phone and then the doors are locked with no visible way to unlock them. It's like we are in some parallel universe," Sammy said.

"Wait, Sammy you said Parallel Universe," I said as a thought came into my head. "Like an alternate reality or something?" I asked. The answer was right there, but how I wondered.

"Yes, why?" she asked. "Why do you think it is something out of one your fiction novels Natasha? Come on, really. "It's called fiction because it's not real," Sammy sneered with annoyance at my thoughts. She really didn't like things she didn't understand.

"What if, when we turned down that road, we entered a parallel universe, when the snow storm began," I said. I know it sounds crazy, but think about it; the blizzard out of nowhere, it didn't even show up on the weather radar, then the freaky messages when we entered the house, and now we are locked inside and the snow is gone nowhere to be seen," I said pointing out the window.

"Yeah right Natasha. Are you still drunk?" Ivy snapped. "Just because you write it, doesn't mean it can actually happen," Ivy said full of anger. She didn't like the unknown either, and since I was the only one with a wild imagination they were shutting down thought.

"I understand you guys think I am crazy, and have my wild imagination, but we all can see there is something abnormal going on. I'm not saying its black magic or anything like that," I said trying to make them understand I wasn't enjoying this. "All I think is that there is something we don't know, and we need to find out what it is. It holds the key to getting out of here," I said calmly.

"Ivy, you said your husband might be behind this. Why do you think he would play a cruel joke on us?" I asked. "Do you think he could possibly be behind this?" I asked cautiously. I really didn't want to start any problems; we were all very upset and our minds were going in every direction possible, so I needed to tread lightly on accusing, or suggestions

"I don't know. He has a twisted sense of humor. He is always playing stupid jokes on people," she said nonchalantly. "Honestly, I don't think he would be smart enough to follow us, and change all the locks on the doors, without us seeing him," she said. "He is a very intelligent man, but this kind of trickery, is one from someone into witchcraft or black magic," she said without realizing she was proving my theory. "Ok, so maybe Natasha is right," Ivy snapped.

"Ok, so we need figure out how someone could have done this," I said. "If we figure out what caused this, then maybe we will know the source, and find a way out," I said hoping to bring them some peace or comfort.

"Sammy, Sammy are you ok?" Trish screamed. "You guys look! It's Sammy; she's out cold and won't move. She has a pulse and is breathing normal, but she is comatose," Trish cried as she knelt down next to Sammy on the floor, crying and shaking her to get her to wake up.

"She was fine a minute ago," I said kneeling down next to her. "Did she say anything or do anything before she went down?" I asked hoping Trish would have the answer. She always knew the answer.

"No she was just sitting here listening to everything and the next thing I knew, she was out," Trish cried. "Oh, please be ok Sammy, please be ok," Trish cried as she held her.

"Really, you guys what is going on?" I asked. "We need to call the police," I said. When I dialed 911, all I got was a busy signal. How could 911 be busy?" I asked.

"It can't be," Ivy said with fear in her voice. "It would be pointless to call the cops if there is a busy signal," Ivy said looking very scared and paralyzed by fear.

"Ok, I will text my husband. He will help," I said as I began to text Seth. "It won't go through," I cried. "It said service unavailable." "Ok, we need to lay Sammy down somewhere safe," I said. "The couch, in here, so we are near her," I said, "She will be comfortable and safe," I said, really unsure if that was true.

"Natasha, she's gone," Trish said. "She's not here anymore. Her body is gone-it vanished. Oh no we are all going to die," Trish scream franticly.

"What?" I asked as I spun around to see that Sammy had vanished. "Where did she go? Who took her?" I cried as I turned around to see what we may have missed. "Trish you need to get a hold of yourself right now," I demanded as I saw her spinning in circles, panicking.

"I don't know, but this is beginning to feel like something dark and evil," Ivy said. "How can she be awake one minute, and asleep the next, and then just gone poof into thin air," Ivy said. I could see the confusion in her eyes; she was on the brink of breaking.

CHAPTER 3

The Evil Among Us

"Ivy, what have your parents told you about this place?" I asked "Have they told you what happened to your great grandfather? Have they ever mentioned this place, or anything that can help?" I demanded. "Ivy, you have to remember if was there anything they told you that can help us. I pushed to find the answer.

"I don't think there is anything my family ever mentioned him after his accident," she said. "All I remember is that we used to come here every weekend in the winter on our way to the lodge, and then one time my parents just drove right by, and I never saw my great grandfather again," she said.

I couldn't help but notice the sorrow in her voice, it was like it just hit her, how much she loved to come up here, and how she loved him. "Ok, Ivy. Did they say why they stopped coming here? Did he die, or something?" I asked hoping she could help me figure this out "Ivy, you have to remember something. People don't just stop doing something, and never speak of it again," I said.

"I don't know. All I remember is there was an accident, and my parents received a phone call in the middle night. I remember it woke me up, and I stood at the top of stairs, trying to understand what they were saying, but nothing made sense," she said.

"What was the accident?" I demanded. I was trying not to be pushy and absurd to his memory, but we needed to know was going on. We needed answers to this unbelievable nightmare where nothing makes sense, things aren't real and what is and what isn't. "Ivy, is there any information in the house that will help us; a diary or a journal, something we can use to help us figure this out?" I asked a little bit calmer.

"There is a journal. He used to keep it next to his bed, and every night he would write in it. I remember he used to tell me 'One day, all my knowledge and experiences will save you. My life is here in this book. It holds more power than you will know," she said. "I always thought he meant he was going to have it published, so the world would know the life he lived," she said.

"What did he mean-more power?" I asked. "Maybe he was trying to tell you something. Maybe there is something in his journal that will help us," I said hoping she would agree.

"Ok, you two are driving me crazy. Ivy, go get that stupid journal and Natasha what is with all the questions?" Trish demanded. "This is stupid. What do you think is going on here?" she asked. "There is some stupid person messing with our minds, making us believe that we are going to die. There are using a cell phone, it's not a ghost of the technology," Trish snapped.

"She is right," I said. "Maybe it's a neighbor or an enemy of your great grandfather," I said realizing that the unknown was making my imagination run wild. *I guess all those fiction novels have my mind out of reality*, I thought. "Ok, so Ivy, go get the journal. Trish I am sorry. I guess I am being a little dramatic," I said. "I am just scared. First we receive a threatening message, then nothing, and then another one, and now we have Sammy who has vanished into thin air," I said trying to make her understand why I was acting so crazy.

"Natasha, I understand. Believe me. This is all way too weird for me. I was never into horror flicks, and now we are stuck in someone else's horror flick. I am terrified, but we need to stay calm," she said. "Maybe there is some truth to your theory, but I am not ready to realize we are trapped by black magic or something that isn't real," she said with fear in her words.

"Hey, I have the journal," Ivy came running in and said. "It is really old, and hard to read, but there is something interesting in it, and I think it can help us," she said. "You guys are not going to believe this," she said with a little more excitement than I would have imagined.

"What does it say?" I asked. "Does it say anything about the accident?" I asked. I couldn't hold back all my questions. The suspense was killing me.

"Natasha get a hold of yourself," she snapped. "Natasha, you were right. There is something dark and evil going on here," she said.

"We can fix this, all we need to do is figure out how to get out of here," I cried. I couldn't help it, I was terrified, all of this seems like something out of a creepy horror novel, I thought. "Oh no, what if I never see Seth and Jack again," I cried. "I have to find a way out of here," I cried.

"Stop, we are not going to die, it's a parallel universe," Ivy said very calmly. There was an accident, but my grandfather didn't die. He found something in the attic and look," she said.

'Today was the day, I finally found it. The warlock's black stick. It was hidden under the third layer of the floor *board next to the chest in the attic. If I can find the candle and book, I might be able to break the curse that lies beneath the bricks of the house. I called my grandson to tell him that I had finally found it. He and I had searched the house from top to bottom when he was boy. I thought our curse was finally over; but I when I told him, he told me I was chasing something dark and evil and I had thrown away my life. The words hurt so bad, it was like a dagger to my heart. My life has been a dark one- strapped to the curse. One day it's sunny and bright and the next it's dark and evil. He used to understand, but now he thinks I am just a crazy old man, and he is sending the doctor over in the morning. He wants me committed. I have spent my life protecting people from this evil, and now it will be sent free. If I am gone the warlock will be free to prey on the guests of the mansion. I hope I can find it by the rise of the sun in the morning, or it will be too late. The curse will trap my great granddaughter. My grandson escaped only because I remained here, but once she steps foot in the door, she is trapped, and the evil will begin.'*

"Oh my goodness, Ivy; your grandfather gave his life and dreams to stay trapped in this nightmare, only to be committed and have the nightmare live," I said. "What was he talking about the curse of the warlock? Warlocks are not real, curses are not real and nothing he said makes any sense," I said; my mind spinning out of control, unable to make sense of what was going on. "Is there anything else in there about the so called warlock, or curse anything on how it started, or what it is about?" I asked, hoping she would know.

"Yes, it's right here in the beginning. I can't believe this is happening. All of this is because of me. I have put you guys in jeopardy. I am so sorry," Ivy said with a shocking level concern and sorrow. It was as if she knew it was real, or something.

"Ivy, this isn't your fault. You didn't know this was going happen," I said. "None of us knew it would. We all thought this was going to be an awesome girl's weekend … just like when we were in college," I said trying to make her feel better. "Maybe we can reverse the curse or something," I said.

"Yeah, I may not believe any of this, but maybe we can fix it. Maybe we finish what your great grandfather started," Trish said. I knew it was hard for her to admit to the reality but she did to help Ivy. "Come on Ivy finish reading, and maybe we can find the answers to this," Trish said.

"Ok, but can we do another shot first? All this has sobered me up fast," Ivy stated. I grabbed the bottle of tequila; we were all going to need it, if we were going to do this. "Ok, cheers," she said, as we each just drank right from the bottle. "Ok, it says the curse was cast years ago, back in the 1800's when a man named Isaac, came across an enchanted book. Inside the book were spells and potions that belonged to a woman named Glory. She was the guardian of all good magic, but once the book was stolen, the man used it for greed, and wealth, and eventually used it as evil to hold the power of all the magic on earth. Glory used the last bit of magic she held to cast a curse on the man who stole it. She cursed him to a life of misery and unstableness, which would eventually lead him to insanity; being trapped in a world invisible to human eye. Once the doors open, the doors would close with no visible way to open them and the curse would live until the stick lit the candle and then book would be returned. But, until then, every blood passed down would live with the curse. When one would be gone, the next in line would live on with the curse," Ivy told us.

"That is crazy, there is no such thing as magic, and especially black magic," Trish said. "Come on you guys you can't honestly think the words of crazy old man are true," she said.

CHAPTER 4

The Journey Begins

"Yes, we do Trish. There is no other explanation to this. Everything that is in this book so far, is true and you know it," I snapped. "How can you sit there and say it's the words of a crazy old man, when you have seen Sammy vanish into thin air, and the doors, window, and every way out possible to taken from us?" I asked bitterly. *I can't believe she is being so cynical to this, when she has witnessed it,* I thought.

"Stop it, you two. This may sound a little farfetched, and unreal, don't fight with each other. We need to figure out how to get out of here," Ivy snapped.

"Ok, I am sorry," Trish said. "I didn't mean to disrespect your grandfather. But you have to admit, this is crazy and if it is real it is telling us we are dead, there's no other outcome. Only then will the curse will leave," Trish said.

"I know you are scared Trish, but we are too. I am not willing to admit defeat .We haven't even begun to see the evil part yet and I am willing to bet that this gets a whole lot worse and if we don't start looking for the missing pieces. I for one have deadlines and a wonderful husband and son to get home to. I will not die here and let this curse live on to hurt Ivy's children," I said confidently.

"Ok then, here's to breaking the curse and getting home to our families," Ivy said holding up that bottle of Tequila again, she sure didn't like facing reality, I thought. We took another drink, and sat there silent for a few moments.

"Ok, so your grandfather said he found the stick in the attic deep in the layers of the floor boards. So let's go to the attic and see if we can the find the book or candle," I said. "I know we are tired and scared, but if we sit here and wait for it, hell is going to come," I said. "I have done a lot of research on curses and fiction things for my novels, and if this is anything I have read up on, we haven't even begun to see the dark side," I said trying to motivate them to find the answers.

"Yes, let's do this," Trish said. "I may not believe in this, but let's try it," Trish continued. "Now we are going to need flash lights, batteries, candles and anything that makes light," she continued.

"Yes. Trish, go to the kitchen and Ivy, go the den. I will look in the other rooms to find anything we can use," I said. As we wandered through the house looking for anything we could use, I couldn't help but really wish I was still at with Seth and Jack and how I missed them. I made a promise to myself at that moment to get us out of here and return to them. They were my life, and I promised that I would make time to do the things I didn't before. I didn't realize I was crying until I felt my tear streaked cheeks, and noticed my eye lashes were drenched by my tears. *Get a hold of yourself Natasha I demanded to myself. There is no time for sorrow*, I thought. I kept searching.

"Trish, Natasha, did you find anything?" I heard Ivy yell. As we all met back in the living room, each of us, had a few items in our hands that we could use, and flash lights.

"Ok, let's go the attic," Ivy said with fear dripping off every word.

"Why don't we use these to try and break a window first?" Trish asked afraid of what we may find in the attic. Here follow me, the glass looks to be only double paned. We could probably break it with a chair or something," she said.

Ivy grabbed the solid oak chair and with all her strength she hit the window with it. The chair went flying into pieces, and the window remained untouched. That was weird. Not even a dent. I said, "Hey I have message. It's him!" I gasped. It read-Bad move. "What does that mean?" I asked as I read the message. As the words came out of my month, a gust of wind came blowing through the house.

"How is there wind in the house?" I screamed as we were all clutching to something heavy so we wouldn't blow away. "Look!" I screamed as I looked out the window to my right. It's beautiful looking. The sun is shining there's palm trees, and is that the ocean I see? What in the world is going on?" I cried.

"We need to get out of this room," I cried as I let go of the couch, and reached for Ivy's hand. "Take my hand Ivy." "Where is Trish?" I screamed. We looked around and she was nowhere to be seen. "We need to get out of here," I cried.

We struggled against the wind, trying to grab a hold of the doorway, and pull ourselves out of the room. As we pulled with all our might, we managed to get on the other side of the wall. "What was that?" I cried.

"I don't know, but I am not going stick around and find out," Ivy said. "Hey what is that?" she asked as she seen a newspaper lying on the floor. She reached down and grabbed it. On the front page was a picture of us four, and the headline read-'A girls weekend ended in the death of four young women, while on the slopes, a freak avalanche demolished the lodge and the lives of these four bright women.' "What the hell?" Ivy screamed.

"We never went to the lodge," I said confused. "It's the curse. It's messing with us," I screamed. "We need to get to the attic," I said as we raced for the stairs. As we ran up the stairs, I turned to look behind me, and the stairs began to crumble with every step. "Hurry Ivy," I screamed as I saw that.

"In here!" Ivy cried, as we ducked into a crawl space behind a picture. "There are many of these through the house," she said. "Maybe we can get to the attic from them," she said. It wasn't a bad idea I thought. I couldn't help but feel terrified by the sight of that paper. I hoped it was a fake. "Damn it," Ivy said when we reached the end of the tunnel.

"What is it Ivy?" I asked hoping it wasn't more bad news. I didn't much like the idea of crawling in the crawl spaces of a possessed house; I didn't much like doing it in any house. I had never in all my wildest dreams believed something like this could actually happen; all of this seemed so fake-like we were just in a bad dream or something.

"This is stuck. I can't get it open," Ivy said. "There is another crawl space that leads directly to the attic, and if I could get this hatch door open, we could take it to get there, but this stupid house has us locked in," Ivy ranted. "I hate this. Nothing makes any sense. Anything I used to know about this house is no longer that way, all because of a stupid curse," Ivy kept ranting.

I couldn't help but feel sorry for her; she blamed herself for all of this. If she hadn't ~~of~~ said take that dirt road, we would all be together, sipping our wine, in front of the fireplace right now, I thought. I actually blamed her a little, but regardless of fault, or what happened that led us to this place, we were in grave danger, if we didn't get out of this crawl space, I thought. "Ivy come on, we need to get through this. If we sit here whining and complaining about the door, we are surely going to die in here, from our own imagination," I said hoping she would relax and think clearly.

"Well, I don't know what you want me to do. I keep messing with this damn door, and it's stuck," she screamed. I know you blame me. I blame myself for this. I know this is all my fault, but I know how to fix this," Ivy cried as the tears began to stream down her cheeks. She was trying so hard to stay strong, and get us out of this mess, and find Trish and Sammy. The mental strain on her finally made her snap.

"Yes, I blame you for making us take that so called short cut, but as far as everything else goes, I do not blame you. You had no idea this would happen," I said. "You didn't do any of this, so stop feeling sorry for yourself, and help me," I ordered. Tough love was the only love she knew. She was never the mushy type; she was always the one pushing us to go further than we could, and now it was my turn to push her.

"Ok, let's try it together," she offered. We both struggled with the hatch for a few minutes, and it finally cracked. "Hey, it's working," Ivy cried with excitement. "Finally something is going our way," she cried.

"Ok, now I am going to hold it open. You slip out, then I will slip out after you," I said. It seemed so nice to actually have a plan in mind now. "Once you are through, then I will be right behind you-so hurry before the house figures out our plan," I ordered. I couldn't believe the words I was saying, "Before the house figures out what we are doing".

"Ok, come on Natasha," Ivy said as she slipped through the hatch. "I can't believe that worked," Ivy went about saying as I was trying to get through the hatch. "Natasha hurry! It's slipping," Ivy cried.

"I'm out," I cried as I slipped out just in time before it closed. "That was close," I said, realizing how heavy the door was as it slammed shut, almost landing on my foot. "Now, where do we go?" I asked hoping she had a plan, because I didn't have a clue where to go now.

"There is another crawl space, on the other side of that painting. I am warning you-it's very creepy, and I have no idea what we will find behind it," she said. The sound of her words terrified me; all I could think of was giant spiders, and paranormal bugs crawling through there. "Stop freaking yourself out. It will be fine. We will do this together. We just need to stay calm," she said.

Why are you so calm? You have been freaking out, and now you are just totally calm and collected. What's up? You have a plan don't you?" I asked. I couldn't help but feel calmer myself, as she I talked to her.

"I do have a plan, but I need you to trust me," Ivy said. "I can't tell you my plan, I just need you to follow me-and believe me when I say everything is going to be alright," she said.

I wasn't sure what she meant by that, but I had no one else to trust; and if she thought she could get us out, I really had no other option. "Ok, I trust you," I reluctantly said. I couldn't help but being somewhat afraid of what she had in mind, after all the plans she had in the past normally led to her calling her dad for money to bail us out of some situation or another.

"Natasha, I know I have messed up in the past with my hair brain ideas, but I know this is going to work. We just need to get to the attic," Ivy stated. "I am not promising this is going to get us out of here, but I am promising it should help us find some answers," she continued.

I couldn't help but be intrigued by her right now. She really had an idea. I only wish I knew what it was. "Ok, so what do I need to do?" I asked almost afraid of what she might say. "Do I need anything, or something? I asked." "I know you said trust, but I really can't handle not knowing what is going on," I said hoping she would understand, and not think I didn't trust her. I wish this nightmare would be over already, so I can go home to my family, I thought.

"No, just follow me, I will tell you what I need when I need it," Ivy said. As we walked through a very narrow crawl space Ivy had a shocking level of calmness to her, and it made me feel better. I am not sure why she was so calm, but it was nice to see her in control.

ASA Publishing Company

CHAPTER 5

Finding the path to the end

Natasha, have you ever heard of anything like this actually happening before? Not a story made up to frighten people?" Ivy asked. I am only asking, because I know you do research on the stuff you write, before you write it, she said.

I could tell she was hoping I had answer or an idea to help us find a way out of here. "Actually, I have. I did read something about something similar that happened in a little town in China. But it was a very long time ago; back when they believed you were a witch if you did something that was unexplainable, and when they mummified people," I said hoping to redirect her curiosity.

"What happened?" she asked. "Maybe we can get an idea from it," she said hoping I would give her the answers to this one- but the outcome of that was horrifying, and if I tell her, she might freak out, I thought,

"Ivy, it was really long ago. I doubt that anything they used could help us," I said trying to get her to stop asking. Things were bad enough as it was and there was no reason to scare her into thinking we were going to live like this forever.

"You are a terrible liar, and you always have been," Ivy said sternly. "I know there is something you aren't telling me. Come on, how bad can it be? We are creeping through a very narrow crawl space, unsure of what lies behind the corner," she said defiantly. It was bad wasn't it?" she asked skeptically.

"You are right. There's something I am not telling you; only because what is the point in making us more frightened than we already are," I said. "If I tell you the story, it is only going to scare you," I said warning her that it wasn't good.

"Just tell me already," she said, the curiosity was killing her. "I understand it was bad, but that doesn't mean it will be bad for us," she whined. "Come on. What's the worst that can happen? It makes me even more determined to find the answers and get out of here," she said.

"Ok. Legend has it a long time ago, in a time that we've never heard of, a family was brutally murdered in their home, but they never found the bodies of the two children, they were twins a boy and girl," I said as we kept walking throw the narrow crawl space.

"That's it? That's all you are going to tell me?" Ivy whined. She loved horror movies; she loved suspense, which is why she played her fair share of practical jokes on people.

"Come on. What happened next?" she asked again.

"Ok. The legend says that the children we trapped inside the house. They never actually died but were kept prisoner by the evil spirit of the man who killed their family," I said. "Folks who lived nearby said that a curse was put upon the house and that whoever stepped inside the house was forever trapped. Many people entered and never returned. It says they are trapped for all of eternity living in a world where they see it all, but no sees them. They never die and they live day to day, not knowing what each day will bring," I said as I lowered head, realizing that I may never see my family again.

"Oh my goodness, that is terrible. Could you imagine living like that?" she asked realizing what we were up against. "Well it's a good thing that is not going to happen to us," Ivy said with arrogance.

Normally, I would have called her out on being arrogant, but maybe that's what we need to be. *That might just be the trick to getting out of here*, I thought. "I hope your right Ivy, because I will never forgive myself or this house if I leave my son motherless, and make Seth a widow," I said full of anger. I tried not to get angry, but it was boiling up inside me, maybe it's what I need to get back to my family, I thought.

"Natasha, I promise we are getting out of here alive-even Trish and Sammy," Ivy said. "The curse dies by the hand of me, and I don't care what I have to do," she said with vengeance dripping off her words.

"I know if any two people can do it, it is going to be us. We have the determination to do it," I said. "Look how many times we have gotten into some pretty messy situations, and managed to come out of it," I said, trying to convince myself.

"Hey here it is!" Ivy said with excitement. "We have reached the attic. Now all we need to do is get this door open," she cried as she pushed and pulled to get it to move. "It's stuck, damn it," she cried as she tried some more and had no luck.

"Hey relax. Let's try this together," I offered before she had a moment of freak out. We pushed and pried but no luck. I watched the door as we pushed again, and I noticed that it would move, but there was something holding it shut.

"Hey stop Ivy, stop pushing," I said as I watched the door.

"If we don't push we will never get out here, so come one help me push," she cried. She was scared that we were going to be stuck inside the crawl space forever. Her imagination was running wild.

"Look. Watch the door as we push," I said and pushed really hard on the door. "There is something or someone on the other side that is blocking it," I said, hoping she would listen and understand. We need to figure out what is blocking it, I said calmly.

"Hey what if we charge it, and push without stopping, it would be persistent force. It might work," she suggested. "I know it sounds stupid, but the force of both of us, could move it, if we do it together," she said hoping I would agree.

"Ok, that might work, I said. You're right about persistent force. If we do it as one, both our strength and determination might just do the trick," I said. I grabbed her hand as we backed up. "Ok. On the count of three we are going charge that door, but don't stop pushing once we start," I said. I wasn't sure if this was going to work, but at the moment it sounded like the best chance we had of getting out of this creepy crawl space.

"One, two, and three," I said and we ran towards the door, hoping once we hit the door, it would come loose, and set us free from this crawl space. "AAIEE," I screamed as we connected with the door, it felt like something just sliced my arm clean off. I wanted to continue pushing, but the pain was so bad I couldn't, all I could was slide down the door to the floor.

"What happened, Natasha?" Ivy screamed as she watched me fall to floor in slow motion. "You are bleeding Natasha." Ivy cried as panic seized her. "You are losing a lot of blood!" she cried.

"I don't know what happened, I was running and then it felt like something cut me," I said trying to stand up, but not succeeding. Give me your hand, I ordered. I need to get up." I said as I reached for her hand and stood up. "Ivy, I think it's broke, or the muscle has been severed," I said as I began to tremble from the pain.

"Oh no, what are we going to do?!" Ivy cried. Panic had overcome her, and she was losing it. "We are stuck, we are never getting out of here," she cried. "We are going to be stuck forever in this parallel universe and we are never going to see our families again," she cried.

"That's it!" I cried as my hand connected her cheek. "Get a hold of yourself Ivy! "We don't have time for the dramatics. I am not going to die in here, and I am certainly not letting a little scratch keep from my family," I said firmly, hoping she would get the message, and stop freaking out. "If you want to freak out, and panic, then do it another time. I am not going to tolerate it at this moment," I ordered.

CHAPTER 6

The Calm before the Storm

"Sorry," she said as she rubbed her cheek, where I had slapped her. I felt bad for slapping her, but she needed a reality check. "I didn't mean to lose it, but you are hurt and I can't lose you," she said as the tears streaked her face.

"I am sorry I slapped you. I just didn't know any other way to get you to listen," I said hoping she wasn't mad. "I know you are scared and so am I. But fear is only as strong as we let it be. We need to use that fear as motivation to get out of here and back to our families," I said.

"Ok let's do this," she said as she wiped her tears away. "We need to get your arm fixed right now," she said as took her bra off and began to rip the seams.

"What are you doing?" I asked puzzled by her sudden change of mood.

"You need clean dressings on the wound, and who knows what is on our clothes, she said. This is a very expensive push up bra, and it has special features," she said laughing. "You see, the liner is sweat proof, so I never have to worry about being sweaty," she said as she pulled the liner out of it, "and the inside liner is total sterile," she said with a smile.

"The straps are also removable, and fully adjustable, so we can make it any size," she said as she pulled the straps off. "Now give me your arm," she ordered.

I wasn't sure if I trusted her as a doctor. She failed biology and health class, but she seemed very sure of herself. "Are you sure this will work?" I asked skeptically as I handed her my arm. I really enjoy both arms, I said with a giggle. "Here, we can use my button up shirt as a sling when you're done," I said handing her my shirt.

"Perfect," she said as she took the shirt from me. "Ok, now give me the bottle of tequila," she ordered. I couldn't imagine why she wanted the tequila, but I handed it to her anyways. She took a really big gulp, and handed it back to me. Now take a drink, she ordered.

"Ok. Why do we both need to be drunk for this?" I asked. I couldn't help but feel terrified by the sight of confidence in what she was doing. "You are never this calm and confident," I said trying to figure out what she had in mind.

"Ok, take a really big drink and then take another really big drink-but don't swallow until I tell you to," she ordered. "This is going to hurt, but you need to trust me, and do it," she said.

I had no choice but to listen to her, she really seemed to know what she was doing. I took a drink, then I took another one but held it, and handed her back the bottle. I could feel the tequila burning my mouth; it was like the original flavor of Listerine, the yucky kind.

"Now on the count of three swallow, and stay really still," she said. I watched her tie a bra strap around my arm above the cut. "Now, one, two three swallow," she ordered as she poured the tequila into my wound, and I swallowed.

The pain was horrible, but it only lasted for a moment. "Tequila is alcohol and hopefully it cleaned out anything that can cause an infection," she said as she finished putting my arm in a sling. "I know it hurt but that is why I wanted you to swallow at the same time, it was more or less a distraction," and she said expecting me to be ready to fight.

"Well, it worked" I said. "I am not sure what was worse the drink or the pain," I said laughing. "Thank you for doing that. I have never seen you so sure of yourself; it was a nice change," I said, grateful for her determination.

"Ok, we need to get out of here now," she said. "So this time we need to do it as one. Hug me, and use your bad arm to push. The pain will give you more motivation," she ordered. "That will help us push with everything we have," she said hugging me. "Now on the count of three; ONE, TWO, THREE!" she said as we ran as one to the door.

"Hey! It worked!" I yelled as we laid there on the floor of the other side, but it didn't seem like we even hit the door. It was as if it just opened. It hurt when we hit the floor. The pain was worth it to be out of that crawl space.

"Natasha how is your arm?" Ivy asked. "If you want, you can sit down and take it easy while I look this chest for anything that might help us," she offered. She could tell I was in pain, but didn't want to let me know it was noticeable. "If you want you can check the floor boards," she said watching the expression on my face change as she pointed at my arm.

"I am alright. I will check the floor boards, while you look in the chest," I said hoping to find our answers as soon as possible. I grabbed the screw driver that I saw sitting on a table and began checking the floor boards.

We kept very silent while we were looking for the answers, both of us was terrified at the thought of what the house had in store. Although we were silent, we kept glancing at each other, just to make sure the other was still there, neither of us, wanted to face this alone.

"Have you found anything yet?" Ivy asked. She knew I didn't but the silence was driving her crazy, I could tell. "I haven't found anything in the chest. There is a lot of really old stuff in here, but nothing good yet," she said.

"The floor boards are clean." I said. "There isn't anything here, but I am going to check the walls," I said as I got up and went to the wall to my right. I began tapping, trying to find a hollow spot.

"Hey I have something," Ivy hollered as she pulled out a book. "It's a book that has a lock on it," she said looking at it very intently.

I began to walk over to her and my phone started going off. A message! I cried hoping it was from my husband. It's from the house again, I cried as I struggled to bring myself to open the message. "Oh my God!" I screamed as I opened it the message. "It's a picture!" I cried and dropped my phone.

"Natasha what is it?" Ivy cried as she saw the look fear on my face. "Natasha, talk to me," she ordered as I stood there unable to move or speak. Ivy picked up the phone, and screamed at the sight of Trish and Sammy trapped inside the walls. They were all around us, but we couldn't see them. They were inside the walls, just like the curse said. They were never going to return. "Natasha, come on we need to figure out what is going on and get into this book, Ivy cried. Damn it Natasha!" she said and smacked me across the face, just as I had done to her earlier.

"I am sorry, but I can't handle the sight of them trapped like this forever," I said as the tears streamed from my face. "I am sorry. I am trying to keep it together, but it's too hard. I can't bear to think of never seeing them or my family again." I couldn't help the tears from falling. All I wanted was to get out of this nightmare.

"Natasha, I understand. But giving up, and letting the curse win, is really not the best solution," Ivy said as she sat with me, and hugged me. "I promise you-I will make sure that you get out of here and back to your family, and I promise I will save Trish and Sammy," she said. "Now come on. Let's open this book, and figure out how to get home," Ivy ordered as she stood up, and helped me.

"I think we need a key," Ivy said as she tried to open the book, and it wouldn't open. "Imagine that something else that is locked and unavailable for us to open," I said and laughed. "I am going to look in the chest to see if it's in here, even though I would bet my money it's not," she said still laughing.

CHAPTER 7

Secrets Unveiled

"Ivy, look at this lock," I said as I began to remember something she said. "Do you still wear that locket your great grandfather gave when you were a little girl?" I asked. "If you look at this lock, there is a strong resemblance to your locket," I said as I blew the dust away, and read the name 'Secret of what lies beneath'. "Hey, did you read the title of this book?" I asked, noticing it has serious similarities to our nightmare.

"Yeah, I have my locket, but it's in my bag downstairs," she said. "I read part of the title. It was something about secrets, she said as she walked over to me and looked back at the lock. "Hey, that does look like my locket. The emblem is almost the same," she said. "I see that you are thinking my locket could be the key," she said as her eyes got bright.

"Yes. Now do you remember the story behind the locket?" I asked hoping she would remember if there was some importance or special power to it. I was really hoping that things were starting to look up.

"I don't recall any story behind it, except that it has been passed down from generation to generation, and my grandfather thought it would help keep me close to the family heritage," she said, realizing what she said. "I bet that is what he meant by that. He wanted to keep me close to the truth, so if I was ever here, I could do it," she said.

"If that is the case, why would he give you the key to the book that has cursed the house?" I asked puzzled by the ways of her family. "Think about it. In his journal he said he was close to finding the truth, but he couldn't because your dad was having him committed. But when they came to get him, he was gone. He had disappeared, and was never seen again," I said trying to put the pieces together.

"My grandfather never gave me the locket in person. After he disappeared I received it in the mail, for Christmas, and that's just what the note said," she said puzzled as well, by the story. "Maybe, my grandfather sent it to me from beyond. Maybe he is stuck inside the house," she said putting pieces together.

I hated to think it, but it might be true, I thought. "Ok, so we need to get to the locket, and pray like hell it works," dreading to go back through the crawl spaces. "Do we have to use the crawl spaces?" I asked, hoping she would say no, and have a better idea.

"Actually, Natasha we can't use the crawl spaces for the rooms. We would get so turned around it's not even funny," she said. "Do you remember what happened to the stairs when we were walking up them?" she asked.

I did remember. "That is a problem. How are we going to get back downstairs, the stairs are gone?" I asked, dreading her answer even more. I tried to think of a suggestion but I had none.

"We could try rope, she said as she grabbed a huge thick rope. We can tie it the wall, and slide down it," she said. "I know it sounds crazy but it might be our only option," she said trying to convince me.

"That is crazy. You want us to slide down an old rope, and hope the rope or house doesn't kill us," I said disgusted by the idea of it. "We have no idea what this house can do to us. I don't like that idea," I said. "If we use a rope to get to the main floor, in a house that is possessed by a curse, and to add to it, the house sees everything we do, what do you think the house is going to do to us?" I added to emphasize my point.

"What other choice do we have? We can stay up here, and wait for the house to suck us in as well, or try to get out of here," she said. "I understand it's very risky, but everything we are doing is risky. We crawled through many tiny crawl spaces, and managed to get this far," she said.

She was right. Everything we had done, had death or being trapped dangling from it. If there was a way out it was going to take courage, and strength. "Ok, so if we do this, how are we going to tie the rope to the wall, and climb down?" I can only use my one arm," I said remembering the crawl space. "Also, how do we know the wall will hold us?" I asked.

"We don't know if the wall will hold us, or even if the rope will hold up. It's a really old house, and so far we can't trust anything. But what other options do we have? I want to get Trish and Sammy out here and go home," Ivy stated.

I wanted to trust her on this one, but the fear of the unknown was stopping me. "Ivy, do you even understand what you are asking of us?" I cried hoping she would realize that I physically could not climb now a rope. "Ivy, look at me. I am only able to have use of one arm right now and I can't hold my weight up with one arm. I will lose my strength fast and fall," I stated as I pointed to my arm, that had a small stream of blood trailing from it.

"Natasha, I understand that. But we are going to do it together, and use a harness," she cried holding a ragged old harness she found in the chest. "You see, if we use this harness I can strap you to the rope, and then you can help me as I climb us down," she said.

Her idea was better than I had thought, but that harness looked as if it were going to fall apart. "Ok Ivy, say we do use that harness, how you know it will hold us?" I asked looking at it. "It's really old, and probably hasn't been used in centuries," I said.

"I know, but what other choice do we have? Stay up here and wait?" she cried. I could tell she was getting impatient with my lack wanting to do it. "Look, do you have another idea, because I am open to any idea at this point? But I am not going to wait and see!" she stated defiantly.

"What if we use that rope, and that big crate, we can put those quilts in it, so if it does break we have something to break our fall," I said pointing the big crate. "We could also use that post as a pulley system, so we won't just free fall. We can slowly go down," I suggested.

"Ok, let's do it," she said grabbing the crate, and quilts. "Here, I want you to sit in first and see if I can pull your weight up," Ivy said. "If I can pull your weight then we can both pull our weight together to get to the edge, so we don't have to risk jumping," she said as I stepped into the crate and she hoisted it up. "Ok, I can do it. Come on lets rig this pulley thing up," she ordered.

"Ok," I said and grabbed the rope and hooked it around the post. "Ivy, make sure there is enough padding in that thing. It might be the only thing that stands between us and the ground," I said cautiously.

"Ok, I think we are set. Are you ready Natasha?" Ivy asked with a look of fear in her eyes. "Natasha, I promise no matter what, we will be ok," she said hugging me. "Now get in," she ordered as we pushed the crate to the edge and looked down. Oh wow, there is nothing between us and the ground now, Ivy said as she noticed everything had been demolished, all that was left was a pile of rubble from the stair case.

"Oh wow. That is really freaky," I said by the sight of it. "Ivy we can do this. We have to," I said, to reassure her that it was ok. "Ivy, let's just do it and get it over with. If I wait any longer, I will chicken out," I said as I waited for her to get in.

"Ok," she said as she got in, and began to hoist the crate up and over the edge. "Natasha, try and put your weight to the side and I will put my here so we don't tip," Ivy said. I could tell her courage was slowly diminishing, and being replaced by fear.

"Ivy, we can do this. Just do it nice it slowly," I advised as I looked down. "Whatever you do, don't look down," I said realizing the error of my own ways. I kept fairly still; afraid to move or even breathe. Scared of what the house would do to us.

"Natasha, did you hear that?" Ivy cried. "We are in the middle of this. If we fall it is going to really hurt," she cried. "Natasha, hold on tight," Ivy cried as the crate started swaying back and forth.

"How is it moving? There's no wind," I cried. "It's the house!" I said as I realized what was happening. "It is trying to get the rope off the pulley," I cried. Ivy let go faster. I screamed hoping we could beat the house.

"Natasha, look!" Ivy cried as she looked down. "There is nothing but water," she cried. "I can't swim," Ivy cried as she began to freak out. "Oh no, we are going to drown," she screamed as panic took over her entire body.

"Ivy stop!" I screamed as her panic was causing us to tip. "Ivy, stay still, damn it!" I ordered trying not to freak out. "Oh no," I cried as watched the water turn to a swirling vortex. "Ivy, stay calm and close your eyes," I demanded hoping she wouldn't see what I was witnessing.

"Trish," I screamed as I seen her swirling around in the vortex. "Trish, try to fight it, and reach for me," I cried hoping I could save her. "Ivy, hold the rope," I ordered as I remembered I was wearing a harness.

"Ok," Ivy said as she kept her eyes closed clenched the rope. "Natasha what are you going to do?" she asked as opened her eyes. "Oh my goodness," she screamed when she saw Trish. "Natasha what are we going to do?!" she screamed.

"Relax, I am going to get her," I said trying to be calm. "I am going to climb out and you are going to lower us. While you are doing that, I will try and grab her," I said.

"No, you can't," Ivy cried. "You only have one arm right now and you can't handle her weight and your own," she said.

"No, but I am wearing the harness, so I won't have to," I said grabbing my harness. "Ivy we have no other choice; you can't swim and I can't hold the crate alone. I promise it will be alright," I said as I made my way over the side of the crate. "Ivy, brace yourself and be prepared to steady it back," I ordered.

As I watched my dear friend being whipped and torn through the swirling vortex, I wondered if I would be able to save her, would I have the strength to do it. "Trish!" I screamed as I began to lower myself from the crate. "Trish, grab my hand, reach for me," I screamed. She was there, but it was like she couldn't see or hear me, how can I get her to see me, I wondered.

"Natasha you are going to have to jump in after her. She is in a trance. Nothing is real to her," Ivy yelled from the crate. "Please Natasha, be careful. I don't want to lose you too," she cried.

I knew how scared she was, but I was not about to let one of my best friend be stuck in a place where they live forever in an upside down spiral. Trish had been my friend ever since we were kids, she was family, I couldn't let her down, I thought.

"I'm going in Ivy. Hold that rope as tight as possible. I mean it!" I ordered. She knew how risky this was, but I knew she could do it. *'Give me strength. Give me speed'*, I prayed, not sure to whom at that moment, but I knew someone in that world had the power to help me. I closed my eyes, and there was my son and husband. I had to get her out and get back home to my family. The tears began to fall. They felt like shards of glass hitting my arms.

"Ivy, drop me fast, but hang on tight!" I screamed. Ice formed in my blood as I hit the water. It was arctic feeling, but it was numbing, so that helped. I couldn't feel the pain, inside or out. "Trish," I cried as I seen her spinning rapidly, I reached out trying to touch her, but I couldn't get to her, the harness was restricting me.

"Ivy, I have to take this harness off; but leave it down so I can swim back to it," I cried. I knew this was a bad idea. I was at the mercy of the house. I was in bed with the curse and there was nothing I could do but push harder and faster than the evil rushing to me.

"Natasha no, please don't. You will die," Ivy cried. "Please keep it on. If you get caught in the spiral motion, I won't be able to get you out. I don't know how to swim," Ivy cried. It pained her beyond words to think of losing me.

"Hey, there is a message," Ivy screamed as she looked at my phone. "It's from private again. Oh my goodness, Natasha it says, 'Hanging in the air, holding on by a hair, do you dare, Four come in 2 down, one in the air, and one in my care,' what does that mean?" she cried as she looked down at me.

I had already taken the harness off, and began swimming toward Trish. "Natasha stop! Come back please! The curse is going to take you too," she screamed. I knew I had to keep going. I had only one thing on my mind, and was that bringing us home!

"Trish," I cried as I was inches from her. Grab my hand. Please Trish reach," I cried as I tried to reach out and grab her and she disappeared. I couldn't breathe. I risked everything to swim through this spiral mess, and she disappears. The anger boiled beneath the skin on me, I couldn't control the rage as it came busting out of me.

"Natasha, are you ok?" Ivy asked skeptical as she watched all the water being vaporized, and disappearing. "Natasha, come on talk to me. The water is gone!" she cried. Fear dripped off her every word. The tears fell from her eyes and each tear drop I saw fall from her, made me even angrier.

CHAPTER 8

The Anger from Within

"She disappeared," I muttered unable to speak clearly. "She is gone. The curse has gotten the best of us," I said with vengeance dripping off my tongue like venom.

"Natasha you are scaring me. Are you possessed by the curse, or have you lost your mind?" she cried terrified by the sight of me.

"Ivy, it was a trick. We risked our lives to get to Trish, and when I finally got to her she wasn't real," I said. My tone got deeper as I reached the end of the sentence. "Ivy, do you still have your cigarettes and lighter?" I asked. It had been over five years since I had a cigarette, but I think I was due at this moment. "Please don't tell me no. I need a damn cigarette and a drink of that tequila for what I have planned next," I screamed as if she was arguing with me.

"Natasha, I am not your enemy. I wouldn't tell you no if you asked me for anything. You are terrifying me," she said in a very soft calm voice, afraid to upset me. "Look Natasha, I have no idea what you are planning, but by the look in your eyes, I don't doubt that you will win," she said, scared to even move. "How did you get the water to disappear?" she asked as we both realized we were standing at the front door of the house.

"The house feeds on fear," I snapped realizing what we were up against. "The curse lives by the fear in our hearts, and I am no longer scared. That fear has been replaced by total anger, I said as I smacked her across the face. "Do you feel that Ivy? It's anger. Get mad-be furious, but don't be scared. Don't feel anything but anger," I snapped as I slapped her again, trying to push her to the point of no return.

"Damn it Natasha, stop slapping me. It is really starting to piss me off," she snapped at me. "I swear, if you slap me again, I will snap, I mean it," she declared.

"Good. Now what do you feel?" I asked as I raised my hand to strike her. She grabbed my hand and held it.

"I mean it. Don't," she ordered. "I feel anger, and rage. Are you happy now? We are pissed at each other. Is that what you wanted? Are we are going to spend our time fighting each other, instead of what is really important," she said as she raised her hand and struck me.

"Good. Now focus your anger at the curse, and getting out of here," I said happy that she has reached the rage that I was feeling. "Now let's get that locket and find a way to get back upstairs," I demanded. "You said it was in your bag, in your room. Now move it," I snapped.

"Ok, this way," she said as she led the way. "It looks like nothing has ever happened in here," she said looking at the house, and everything was intact.

"Yeah, it does. See, we can beat this. We will get Trish and Sam, and go home," I said still just as angry as I was before. "There's your bag," I cried as I saw it against the wall. Typical Ivy. She was never one to put things away. She has always been the one to say, 'I'll do it later.'

"That's where I left it," she said with a laugh and reached down to open it. "Here it is," she said lifting up the locket. Come on let's get to the attic," she said. "Why didn't we bring the book down here with us?" she asked.

"We did. It was in the crate," I said as I walked over to the crate that just appeared on the floor. "Things are beginning to get stranger. Why is everything at our fingertips now, when everything was just out of our reach before? Ivy, why are things available now, but five minutes ago they weren't?" I asked, wondering what was going on.

"Another message!" Ivy cried. "I don't want to open it this time. You do it," she said throwing the phone at me. "I am sorry, but I won't be able to control myself if it's something bad," she said.

"Ok. I will," I said as I opened it. It says 'You win. The doors are open.' I repeated it to her, and just as I did, the doors opened and we were free. "This is a trap," I said looking all around me, wondering what on earth was happening.

"Natasha come on, we can leave. Let's do it," Ivy cried. "What are you waiting for?" Ivy cried as she watched me standing there unable to move, unsure of what would happen.

"What about Trish and Sam?" I asked. "I can't leave them here," I said to her. "We all came together and we can't leave without them," I said as I felt my heart break at the thought of losing my best friends. "They are like sisters to me," I said to Ivy who was almost to the door.

"Natasha, if we leave, we can come back with help? Remember the woman who owns the shop just down the road from our favorite coffee shop?" she asked. She practices magic, and knows all about this. We can have her come with us, and then we will know what we are up against," she continued.

"Ok, let's get her," I said reluctantly. I hated the idea of leaving them, but maybe she was right. We needed someone who understands this kind of stuff, and knows how to fix it, or bring peace to the curse. "Ivy, are you sure we should do this?" I asked as I looked back at the house from the doorway.

"Yes, we need to get help, and you need to see your family, and tell Seth. He understands all of this and he could probably help," she said. She knew if she mentioned my family, I wouldn't hesitate about seeing them again.

"Ok," I said, and practically ran out the door. I turned back once we reached the car, and there was Trish standing in the window. "Ivy, look! There they are," I cried as I saw Sammy walked up to the window too. "Ivy, we can't leave them," I cried, as I tried to run back to the door, and Ivy grabbed me.

"Natasha, do you remember what happened when you reached her in the water? She disappeared. This is a trick. Don't fall for it. We need help and now we can get it, so come on, please I am begging you, please Natasha," she cried.

"Ok," I said and reluctantly got in the car. "Ivy you'd better be right. I will never forgive you, if I never see them again," I said with tears falling from eyes, as my heart bled from the idea of never seeing them again.

"Natasha, I promise we will come back for them," Ivy said, as she backed out of the driveway. "Natasha, think of Seth and Jack. They will be waiting for you when you get home," she said trying to make me feel better.

The ride was very quiet, neither of us knowing what to say to help the other. I kept thinking of Trish and Sammy in the window, scared of what will come next, not knowing if they will see us again, thinking we abandoned them to a life of spirals and unknown. I tried to cover the tears that were burning beneath my lids, but one escaped and took a slow turning path down my cheek.

"Natasha, when we get to your house we will tell Seth, and take Jack to your parent's house so he will be safe. Then we will go to that shop, and get some answers," Ivy said.

"Natasha, please don't be mad at me. I know it feels like we abandoned them, but we didn't. We are going back and we will get them," she said putting her hand on mine.

"I know. I am not mad at you. I am just sad, and worried. I will never forgive myself if they never get out," I said. "I don't blame you, or anyone. It's just hard to believe that after all that we've been through, we're going back. I hope Seth doesn't think we are crazy or drunk," I said.

"Well it looks like they are home," she said as we pulled in my driveway. I was so happy to be home, but I was terrified by what was going to happen next. "Natasha, just be happy you got your family back. We will get them, but right now go kiss your man, and hug your baby," Ivy said as she put the car in park.

I practically leaped out of the car, and ran to the door, "Seth honey, I am home," I yelled as I opened the door. "Hey guys, where are you?" I cried as walked through the house looking for them. Where are they, I wondered as I went out the sliding door to see if they were out back.

"Natasha, wait!" Ivy cried and came running up. "Look there's another message from private," she said holding up the phone. I felt my heart fall to my feet. I was paralyzed by what it was going to say. "Natasha, I am so sorry," Ivy said as she handed me the phone.

'What is right is no longer in sight. They have gone to the light. You will have to fight to get back what is right. Go back or they will never see light,' the tears poured out of my heart as I read it. The curse had taken my family. "I knew it was a bad idea to leave. Ivy how could you," I screamed. I couldn't feel my legs. I lay there paralyzed.

CHAPTER 9

The Battle

"Natasha, get in the car. We are going to see that woman," Ivy demanded as she grabbed my arm to help me to my feet. I couldn't stand. I lay there unable to speak or move. My family was gone, the curse had them. "Damn it Natasha, this is no time for sorrow. What do you think Seth would do if it were you? Would he lie here in self-pity and sorrow, or would he fight for you, and break the curse at the core?" Ivy said as she grabbed my face to make me listen.

"Ok," I said, as I stood up and walked like a zombie to the car. I felt like the life had been sucked right out me. How can I fight if I can't feel? My heart had been ripped out and cut into pieces. My family was gone, and I didn't have a clue how to get them back.

"Natasha you need to get mad. Get enraged. That is the only way to save to them," Ivy said. "I know you blame me, and that's ok. Blame me as long it gets you mad. I can't do it alone. Please Natasha help me," Ivy said.

She was right. I had to get my family back. I needed to save them, and I needed to get my family back, before it was too late. "Ok, let's go see that woman," I said sternly, I felt the rage building back up. I knew what I needed to do, but it wasn't going to be easy. "Ok, so we need to see this woman and get back to the house before night fall," I demanded. "I refuse to spend one more night away from my family," I said with flames of rage infusing my body with strength.

"Good," Ivy said forcefully. "We will rip apart the curse piece by piece," Ivy boasted. I know she was just trying to make me feel better, but my heart bled. My family was gone and I may never see them again.

"Ivy, I want to be angry, but the only feeling I can feel right now is empty. My world has been stolen from me. How do I get them back? It's not like they were kidnapped. They were stolen by a curse," I said. I would do anything to get them back. "They are all that is important to me. Without them, I might as well be dead," I cried unable to stop the flow of tears that were streaking my face.

"Now Natasha, I am not going to have any of that talk," Ivy demanded as she pulled the car to the side of the road. "Look, if you want to feel sorry for yourself, and cry your tears dry, then be my guest. But, you will do it alone, because I am going to get our friends, your husband and little boy, and I don't need you slowing me down," Ivy snapped. "Your life may look like it's over, but there is hope. We can get them, but not by feeling sorry for ourselves, and giving up. We need to fight, and persevere to win. I will not let that curse take any more people I care about. It has taken so much from family as it is," Ivy said a bit calmer.

"Ok, I am sorry, but I am scared to death right now. I don't want to lose my family," I cried. "Give me two minutes to cry it out and then I will fight to the end to bring them home," I sobbed.

"Ok, Natasha you do what you have to; but in two minutes I am putting the car in drive and we are going to a woman about magic and crap because, I will not let this curse take anyone else I care about," Ivy said holding my hand as to comfort me.

I sobbed, and sobbed. I had to stop. I couldn't find another tear in me, even if I had to. I must have cried them all out. "Ivy, I am ready," I said as I dried my eyes, and blew my nose. "I must get to my family. I have to. Poor Jack is probably scared out of his mind, and Seth is most likely trying to calm him down, but all he keeps saying is he wants mommy," I said as one last tear managed to find its way down my cheek.

"Natasha, I am sure Seth is fine. He is probable making Jack think it's just a game, and there is nothing to worry about. You know Seth never lets himself get lost in anything, and plus he is a very smart guy, he will handle this as if it something he does every day," Ivy said.

"You are probably right. He has a special way with Jack, and he never gets too worked up over things," I said trying to convince myself more than anything.

The rest of the ride was silent; both of us were scared to say anything, in fear of making the situation worse, and it didn't help that the roads were terrible. They were very slushy, and slippery. I tried not to think the worse but it was hard because, all I could think about was never seeing my family again; and I couldn't let that happen.

"Hey, we are here. Are you ready?" Ivy asked. "Come on, we need to know what we are up against," she said as she opened her door and got out. "Are you coming?" she asked as I realized I was still sitting in the car.

"Yeah, I just needed a minute to get it to together," I said as I got out of the car. "Is she even here?" I asked noticed how dark the place looked.

"Yeah, she has to be," Ivy said as she went to the door and knocked really hard. I thought the neighbors could hear it, it was that loud. "Hey please open up," Ivy screamed into the door.

"Ivy, what are you doing?" I asked. "You are going to get everyone in town out here, wondering what the big deal is," I said, looking around to see if someone was watching.

"I don't care. I want to see this woman, and we need her help. So if that means getting the whole damn town out here to help, then so be it," she stated and continued to bang profusely against the door.

"Just a minute," a voice called. "Please stop beating my door, I am coming," the voice said. It was a very soft woman's voice, slightly high pitched but very soothing voice. "What can I do for you?" the woman asked as she opened the door. She was a very short slender woman, with hair down to the top of her butt, and darker than any black I had ever seen, she had a very pale complexion.

"Yes, Miss. Please I need your help," I cried. "We were on our way to a ski resort, but we got snowed in at a possessed house and now our two friends, and my son, and husband have disappeared in that house." I begged her to help.

"Whoa. Wait a minute. Are you telling me a house is possessed and kidnapped your friends and family?" she asked very skeptically.

"Yes," Ivy said before I could say anything. "Look, we are serious, and we don't have much time. May we come in, and talk to you please?" Ivy asked.

The woman, looked very unsure of us, and really didn't want to let us, but I think part of her could see our desperation. "Alright. But I am warning you ... I do practice, and if you try anything, I will turn you into rats," she snapped.

"I promise we won't. We just need you to help, and then we will be on our way," I said, hoping she would listen to us, and not have us committed.

CHAPTER 10

Help Has Arrived – Or Has It...

As we walked in, I could tell she really did practice, and she knew what she was doing. There were cylinders of egg looking things, and spider legs. There was a big canister with what looked like eye balls, in it.

"Ivy, are you sure about this?" I whispered to her. "This woman has lots of weird things, in here, and I bet she is very farouche. Her complexion looks as if it has never seen sunlight," I said very quietly.

"You do know I can hear you, "the woman said. "And yes, I am very farouche. It has been a very long time since I have had a relationship. Most people think I am the devil's mistress, or some other type of devil worshipper." she said.

"Oh I meant no disrespect, or to cast judgment on you. I am sorry." I said realizing that I too, was treating her that way.

"I understand. But you as a writer should be more open minded to things that you don't understand. After all it could make a great story," she said eyeing me intently.

"How did you know I was a writer?" I asked very shocked by her correct accusations, and assumptions of me. "I did not tell you that I was a writer, nor did I give indication that I was," I said, intrigued by her.

"No you did not; but you use words, most don't. Most would say I seemed shy or unsociable, but you used the word farouche, which means shy," she said as she raised her eyebrow at me, as if she were looking past my exterior and into my soul.

"You are right; and again I am sorry, I will not make accusations again," I said.

"Ok, so can we discuss the matter at hand?" Ivy interrupted and asked.

"Of course. I am guessing you are the daughter of wealthy parents, and a wealthy family. Am I right?" she asked looking at Ivy.

"Actually, yes. But what makes you think that?" Ivy asked.

"You are wearing clothing that clearly cost more than my store, inventory included, and you don't like to be ignored," she said.

"Yes, I do wear expensive clothing. But I am not in the mood to play physic. I just want to get our friends and her family out of that damn house and burn it to the ground. It has taken much from my family," Ivy stated. So are you going to help us or not?" she snapped.

"Yes, I am going to help you, and I am sorry about your loss with this house, but burning it to the ground will not help it at all. You need to break the curse, and free the souls that have been taken by the house. This is not going to be easy and you yourself might get stuck in there, and never be able to free it again. Are you guys willing to subject yourselves to that?" she asked with the tone of death.

"No, I am not going to die there. I will walk out with my family," I snapped. "There is no way in hell I am going to let that house or curse win," I stated obstinately. I stood tall and firm, holding my ground. "I am not going to be the reason my family and friends spend eternity in that hell hole."

"Ok, then. You my dear are ready. How about you?" she asked as she looked to Ivy.

"I am with Natasha. I will not let the curse take anyone else in my family, and Natasha and her family are mine as well," she said standing tall. Oh, Sammy and Trish are part of the family. It's a package deal, and Seth knew that when he married her," Ivy said with a laugh.

Ivy was right. "He knew we were a package deal. Get one, get all," I said laughing.

"Alright. First I'll need background information on the house, the curse and all that have been affected by the curse. How it started, and so forth," she said. "Oh, and my name is madam' Lilly, so please call me Lilly," she said.

"Yes, Lilly, thank you" I said unable to control the overwhelming feelings that I was having at the moment: sad, happy, scared or all of the above. "Thank you again Lilly, thank you," I said. "Please call me Natasha and that is Ivy," I said realizing I hadn't introduced myself or Ivy to her yet.

"Of course Natasha, but I am not promising a positive outcome on this. I wish I could but, with curses, a lot of times it doesn't come out good. More than half come out badly," she said.

"I understand that, but this case has no bad outcome. I will not allow that," I said determined to win. "You see not only am I very motivated, determined and stubborn but, I am also far more competitive, and this is one game I will win," I said hoping she realized how much I needed to be right.

"Ok, first off, do you have any information that could help me like, how the curse was started and where it generates from?" Lilly asked.

"Yes, we have my grandfather's journal and another book that needs my locket to open it. I remembered to grab them as we left the house," Ivy said pulling them out of her bag.

"Oh Ivy, you did? Thank you!" I cried. I had completely forgotten about them, I said hugging her. Ouch, I cried remember the cut on my arm, as we squeezed each other.

"Oh Natasha, we need to get that taken care of," Ivy said. "Excuse me, Lilly do you know how to take care of a nasty cut on her arm?" Ivy asked as she took the pieces of the shirt off my arm.

"I know just the thing to do. Stay put," she said and went to the back.

I couldn't help but be nervous about what she was going to do. "Ivy, thank you," I said. I wanted this nightmare to be over, sooner rather than later.

"Natasha, we are going to get them all out of there, but first we need you to be ok. I don't want that arm to get infected," she said.

"Alright, Natasha. Have a seat. Ivy, I need you to drink this, and then you need to be my nurse," she said.

"Why am I drinking this?" Ivy asked. "Natasha is the one who is injured," she said.

"You both have been put through so much. This will strengthen you and give you a reboot so to speak," she said, handing it to Ivy.

"Ok," Ivy said and drank it; more like slammed it. "That is the worst thing I have ever drank," she gagged.

"Yes, but that might just be the one thing that gives you the strength you need to get through this," she said. "Now Natasha, sit very still. But first, you need to take this in one swallow. Just drink it," she said, handing me a shot of something very dark, almost black. "Please, Natasha, if you don't drink this, then what I do to your arm, will have no point. This medicine will heal it," she said.

I took the shot, and drank it in one gulp. "Ugh this is disgusting!" I said still tasting it in my mouth. What is it?" I asked. "Wait, please don't tell me. I really don't want to know," I said.

"Alright. Now sit very still, and Ivy, hand me that warm wet cloth," Lilly said sternly. She began to light wipe out the wound, and pull the skin back, so it was open, I was very intrigued by her knowledge, and she was very educated on her practice.

"Now, hand me that mucky looking stuff," she ordered. "Quickly please," she said. "Thank you. Sorry to be demanding but this is time sensitive, and I need it to work," she said sincerely. "Now this is going to hurt," she said, and immediately lathered it in the wound, and packed it inside it. It really did hurt but there was something soothing about it. "Now the clear plastic wrap," she ordered. She wrapped it around the wound, and it was amazing, it was actually healing right there in front of us.

"Ivy look, it is healing rapidly," I said completely shocked by what my eyes were seeing. It doesn't hurt, or anything, it's really magic, I said. My eyes must have been bigger than saucers, because I couldn't take them off what I was seeing; it was unbelievable.

"Here now drink this." It's the same thing that she drank, "You need a boost, and this will do it," she said handing me a glass of the same stuff that Ivy drank.

"Ok," I said reluctantly. I drank it as fast as I could. It was just as nasty as the other stuff. "Ugh that is pretty gross too!" I said still trying to get that taste off my tongue.

"Hey, I just got a voicemail," Ivy yelled. "It's from Lance," she said shocked. "Aw, that is sweet. He just wanted to tell me he loves me, have a wonderful trip home and he misses me beyond belief," she said as she listened to the message.

"I guess we all have a reason to get home, now don't we?" I said realizing how happy she was. "We have to get Trish to her Mr. Wonderful. She has been through so much. She deserves the happy ending more than anyone else I can think of," I said remember how happy she was when she told us of her news of getting engaged. "And Sammy has a new promotion to get to," I said remembering how excited she was to get her own assistant. "I miss them so," I said. "On the way to the resort we were all happy and having a good time. Now they are trapped in alternate universe and we are stuck outside of that, trying to get in," I said wishing they were all with me.

"Look, there is no time for self-pity, and sadness. I need you angry and mad at the world. Your anger is the power you have against the house," Lilly said.

"Remember when you got mad, I mean madder than you had ever been, and the water disappeared, and the doors opened?" Ivy said. Get that mad again. No sadness, no sorrow, no self-pity, and no doubt. I need you to be stronger than me. I can't do it if you're weak," Ivy said.

"Ok, I am ready; I am getting my family back," I said. "What do we do first?" I asked more as an order than a question.

"Good, you are ready," Lilly said. "Now where is that journal, and locket book thing?" Lilly asked.

"Here it is," Ivy said as she handed it to Lilly. "If you open up to this page here, you will see what the curse is about," Ivy said opening the book to page we read before.

"Ok, it says the curse was cast years ago, back in the 1800's when a man named Isaac, came across an enchanted book. Inside the book were spells, and potions, the belonged to a woman named Glory who was the guardian of all good magic. But once the book was stolen, the man used it for greed, and wealth, and eventually used it as evil to hold the power of all the magic on earth. Glory used the last bit of magic she held to cast a curse on the man who stole it, and cursed him to a life of misery and unstableness, which would eventually lead him to insanity, being trapped in a world invisible to human eye. Once the doors open, the doors would close, with no visible way to open them and the curse would be live until the stick lit the candle and then book would be returned. But until then every blood passed down would live with the curse, when one would be gone, the next in line would live on with the curse."

"Alright, so I am guessing that you Ivy, are the legacy of this tragedy," Lilly said. "Was there anything about the candle and stick?" she asked puzzled by the riddle belonging to this curse. She sat there silent for a few moments. I could tell she was thinking ... conjuring something in her brain, but what, I wondered.

"What are you thinking?" I asked breaking the silence of room.

"I must see that other book," she said flat toned. It was a very wary tone, no emotion linked to it.

Ivy handed it to her, and the locket. "Come in the back with me please," she said she and got up and walked to the back. We followed her. I couldn't help but feel alarmed by this.

"Why do we need to be in the back for this?" I asked unable to control my curiosity any longer.

"I want to make sure there is no curse linked to opening this book outside the house and this room is enchanted. I put a spell on it to prevent curses and other dark magic from entering," she said.

"Oh, that's good," I said feeling better about the back room now.

"Girls please put these on," she said handing us a necklace. "These are tigers eye emulates, and they protect against dark magic. You may keep them. You will need them," she said. We both did so, unable to speak, or even breathe, as she put the locket in the key on the book. We both watched very closely.

CHAPTER 11

The Answers and Questions

"Get behind me," Lilly yelled as the book began to flip pages, and hover above, all on its own. Lilly began mumbling something. *"Omay, anay, darkness go away. Amay anay, evil among us, disray. Omay, anay, leave that way,"* she repeated over and over until the book, slowly made its way back down to her lap.

Ivy and I sat there still, unable to move, clinging to each other for security, terrified by what we just witnessed. "Ivy, are you alright?" I whispered.

"Yeah, are you?" she asked just as quiet.

"Yeah, that is unreal," I said. "How did it do that?" I asked in a voice just above a whisper.

"It's alright. There is no evil left," Lilly said as she turned the page to the beginning. "I promise, it is alright," she said with a giggle at our childlike reaction to what we had just seen. "Really girls, after everything you went through at the house, you are going to let a levitating book scare you?" she asked with a laugh.

"I guess she's right," I said with a laugh. "We have seen far worse than that," I said looking at Ivy, who was laughing as well.

"Now we don't have much time. According to this, you have a seventy two hour window to get your friends and family out once they have been taken," she said.

"That means we only have about forty-eight, maybe a couple more than that." We have to get a move on this," I said. "What is next?" I asked.

"In order to break to the curse and free the souls, you have to return the book to the candle and light the stick," she said. "There is something missing from this," she said as she turned the page. "There it is. We need a blood relative of Glory's family on the book, and the stick to light the candle, otherwise it won't light, but we also need a blood relative of the man who stole the book," she said. "Ivy, are you a blood relative. Now think back and make sure you are, otherwise we need to find another way," Lilly said.

"I think so, my father wasn't adopted. Neither was my grandfather," she said. Ivy sat there thinking.

"You continue to think and I will read more into this," Lilly said. "Here we go. Here is a family tree," Lilly said as she went down the limbs of the tree. Ivy your name is not on this list, she said.

"Maybe it hasn't been updated," I said hoping that was the case.

"No, there is someone else in her spot. It is a magical book, it will update upon conception," Lilly said. "Do you know anyone by the name Jeannette Samantha Gillian?" she asked.

"Is that Sammy's first name?" I asked. "Sammy has always gone by here middle name, because it was her deceased grandmother's name," I said. "How can that be?" I asked. "Ivy, pay attention. How could Sammy be the legacy, instead of you? Are you two related?" I asked.

"No, the only thing we have in common is our birthdates," Ivy said. "There has got to be a mistake," Ivy snapped.

"No, there is never a mistake in the order of magic. It's beyond the control of humans, so there are no mistakes," Lilly said. "Ivy, please look at this," Lilly said as she showed her the imprints of the words. "This book has never been created by a human ... only magical beings," Lilly said.

"Ok, so if Sammy is the blood relative, how do we get her blood?" I asked tired of wasting time.

"Did she have thing like a used band aide, or Kleenex that she used?" Lilly asked.

"I'm not sure, but maybe if we look in her stuff we can find something," I said.

"If you can find a solid piece of her hair, then I can turn it into her blood," Lilly said. "Alright, we need to gather a few things before we go," Lilly said as she ruffled through some things.

"Are you coming with us?" I asked.

"Yes, I will not let you go in alone. It is too dangerous for the two of you. You have no experience with this," she said as she put some stuff in a little sack type purse. "Here, you will each need this vile. Inside is a potion that will make you magical creatures. It is not permanent, but it lasts forty seventy two hours, so drink it now and on the way I will train you how to use your power," Lilly said.

I was very unsure of drinking a magic potion, but I wasn't about to start arguing with her since she had been right on everything so far. "Ok," I said as I drank the potion, and Ivy did also. "That wasn't really that bad," I said. I thought it would be worse than the others. I didn't feel any different "Ivy do you feel any different?" I asked not really knowing which answer I wanted to hear.

"Not really," she said, "but you are right, that stuff didn't taste bad at all, compared to the other stuff," she said making a face. "Are we supposed to feel differently?" Ivy asked.

"No, you will feel completely normal," Lilly said. "I will show you how to use your powers, just as soon as I finish packing," she said. "Will you two go up front and gather all the potions you find? There is also a dagger that I need as well as the little stone bowl and crusher and some herbs. Just get all of them, and some sage sticks," she said as we walked to the front.

"I wonder why she needs all these herbs and potions? Do you think she is going to betray us Ivy?" I asked. "I don't feel threatened by her. I am just a little worried, because of everything. I guess I am just being paranoid," I said not even waiting for her reply.

"Natasha, don't worry. I have faith in her. She seems to know what she is doing, and if she was going to hurt us, I think she would have done it early," Ivy said.

"Yeah, I guess you're right. I am just letting my imagination get the best of me again. I guess that's what happens when you write mystery novels," I said laughing as we gathered everything she asked for. "Hey Ivy, do you think we should get this?" I asked holding an enchanted candle stick.

"What is it?" she asked. "An enchanted candle stick," she said as she read it. "Sure why not, any extra magic will surely help us right now," she said.

"Are you guys ready?" Lilly came out and asked. "Hey what is that?" she asked as she looked at the stuff in my arms. "What were you planning on doing with a candle labeled enchanted candle stick?" she asked with a laugh.

"We thought we might be able to use it," I said shocked by her reaction. "I am sorry. I didn't mean to do anything wrong," I said.

"No. It's alright, but all you are going to do with this is light it; it's meant to help children get over the fear of the dark," she said laughing. "Everything I asked you to grab is what you need; nothing else," she said as she put the candle back.

"Alright, let's go," Ivy said and went to the door. "Natasha, come on. We must be going. Let's go get our family," Ivy said gesturing to the door.

"Yes, we must hurry, but don't worry, I know a short cut," Lilly said as went outside, and she locked the door behind us. "Get in the car," she ordered.

We did so, but I was beginning to realize she was very bossy for such a little woman. Once we were in the car, we both sat silently waiting for her to tell us what to do next.

"Come on lets go," she snapped. "Good. Now Natasha point to that red light and concentrate really hard, and it will turn green.

We did what she asked and it worked. I was shocked. "What else can we do I asked?"

"No talking, just point and listen," she ordered. "Now concentrate on that sign and point to it, make it change to the road the house is on," she said.

I did it and it changed to our road. "Wow, that is awesome," I said completely shocked.

"Pull over, Ivy," she said. "Now, both of you think really hard about the house, and snap your fingers," she ordered.

We all snapped at the same time, and we were sitting in the driveway in front of the house. Our jaws dropped. "How did we do that?" I asked. I mean, "I didn't even see us move," I said.

"Speed of light," she said. "Now hold on to your bags. Ivy do you have the book and the locket?" she asked.

"Yes, I have it all," she said.

"Good. Now hold on tight to your stuff. We can't risk losing them, but we are going all three of us hold hands, still holding our bags, close our eyes, and chant," 'Dark as night, white as light let the curse lift bright, we thee three come to thee.'

We all closed our eyes, and chanted that. I never felt a thing or saw anything. We opened our eyes and we were in the attic. "Hey, we are in the attic. It must be the safest place in the house," I said realizing that we were not harmed in any way up here.

"Yes, attics are always for good magic, never dark magic, those must be performed in the basement or cellar of a magical house," Lilly said. "Now we need to find Sammy's hair brush or something with her human fibers on it, so I can turn it to blood, and find the candle stick," Lilly said.

"I still don't understand how she is the legacy when I am the child of this," Ivy snapped.

"Ivy, look at this book. What does it say?" Lilly asked showing her the book? You see it does not say your name, it says-"Whoa! The name has changed," Lilly said.

"What? How can that be?" I asked. "Now what are we going to do if it changed?" I asked.

"It doesn't have a name. Only the heir of Sammy," she said. "Sammy must be with child, and she must be passed three months," Lilly said. "You see the book is magic, and it sees when the next heir is conceived. And if there will be a miscarriage, it will not put the name on the list, so Sammy must be with child," she repeated. "Maybe that is why it read her name first because she is pregnant by a blood relative, and it recognized the blood first," Lilly said. "Yeah, but that wouldn't be right. Sammy would still have to carry the blood herself, unless you Ivy are the father of the child," Lilly said with a laugh.

"That is not even funny," Ivy snapped. "I can't be the father, obviously!" she snapped. Ivy didn't like being made fun of at all, even if it was just in fun.

"I am sorry, but magic is never wrong. So, Sammy is the heir." Lilly said.

"Now, how are we going to get the babies blood if it's in Sammy, who is trapped?" I asked. I was beginning to get tired of this nonsense.

"Easy. We use any hair or fiber from Sammy and turn it into blood, and it will recognize the baby's blood, because they share the same blood stream right now," Lilly said. "Enough of the questions girls, we need to find the candle, stick, and a hair or something of Sammy's," Lilly said. "Now both of you think hard about Sammy's belongings and they will appear. Only think of her belongings," Lilly warned.

I thought really hard about Sammy's bag, and cloths she was wearing and they appeared in my lap. "Hey, I have them," I said as I started going through them. "Will this work?" I asked holding up her hair brush.

"Yes, perfect," Lilly said. "Now concentrate on that candle and stick, while I work on the blood," Lilly ordered.

"Hey where is Ivy?" I asked as I turned around and she wasn't there. "Ivy," I yelled. "Ivy, where are you?" I cried. Panic had seized my body. How could I do this without her? I wondered.

"Natasha, stop freaking out. Ivy must have wandered out of this room. She is wearing her emulate so, evil can't get to her," Lilly said. "She isn't hurt. She must be in Sammy's room. Sometimes you can appear where you think of," Lilly said.

"Alright, but I need to find her," I said. Ivy, I called as I looked out the doorway and called her name again.

"What?" I heard her yell. "I'm down here," she said as I looked over the edge. There she was in Sammy's room. "I guess I thought too hard about her room, because that's where I'm at," she said with a laugh.

"Come back up here. I have her bags," I said. Ivy was never the predicable one, I thought. "Please be careful, and don't get hurt," I warned.

"Relax, I am walking up the stairs, she smirked. Ooh, what is going to happen?" she mocked me.

"Ivy, knock it off," I said annoyed by her mocking. "Come on, please?" I asked.

"Natasha, help!" she screamed. Please help, she cried again.

"This better not be a joke," I said as I looked around, "Ivy where are you?" I cried. "Lilly, Ivy's gone!" I cried.

"Show me Ivy," Lilly said in a dark tone. "She is in the staircase," Lilly said puzzled by the sight of her. How did the curse get to her? She has on her amulet." Lilly said. "Did she take off her emulate? Did she, did she?" Lilly cried.

I could see that she was very upset. Her pleasant attitude turned to total anger. "I don't know," I said, completely shocked by her reaction. "Look," I cried and pointed over to her bag, "It's her emulate" I cried and picked it up. The locket is still here too," I said with some relief.

"Damn that girl," Lilly muttered. "She can never just listen can she?" Lilly asked. "Come on, we must hurry," Lilly snapped. "I need you to think really hard about the beginning of this curse. Please, it might bring us closer to finding that candle," Lilly said. "One of the powers you have is seeing the past and future, but I only think about the past. Maybe you can see where it is buried or something," Lilly said. I could tell she was very upset right now.

I closed my eyes, slowly breathing in and out, thinking about what I read about where the curse started. I could see a very large oak tree, with a tire swing hanging from it. There was an old wooden bench seated next to the tree. There, I saw the book, the candle and the stick. They were next to the tree.

"Do you see anything yet?" Lilly asked. "Try not to break your focus, but tell me what you see," she said. If you can't that's alright, just try and keep your focus," she said softly.

Her voice was very in tune with thoughts. "I see an oak tree, with a tire swing, and the book, stick and candle," I said. "There is wooden bench next to the tree," I said still keeping my focus.

"Good. Now see if you can pick them up," Lilly said. "Don't break focus, they are right in front of you. Just try and pick them up carefully," she warned.

I continued to keep my focus. I raised my hand, and reached down just as if they were right in front. I could feel them in my hand and picked them up.

"Do you have them in your hand?" Lilly asked. "Keep your focus, and hand them to me," she said. "Don't break focus-we almost have it. Relax and breathe in and out slowly. You're doing great. Now set them in my hand," Lilly said.

I could feel them in my hand, they were not very heavy, but had a slight weight with an unusual texture to them, like there was writing on them. I kept them in my hand, and placed them in Lilly's hand, still focusing very hard on my surroundings.

"Now, keep your focus. What is happening? Tell me anything about your environment," Lilly asked.

"It's a very bright sunny day and a slight breeze; just enough to tickle your hair," I said. "The birds are chirping, and I hear a chicken some place near.

"Good. You're doing very well. Now try to bring your focus back to me. Follow my voice. You are in the attic of the house on a mission to rescue your family," Lilly said. "Keep coming back to me. We have found the candle and stick and are ready to save them. I just need to do one more thing," she said. Are you with me? If you are and sure you are here in the attic, then open your eyes while holding your emulate around your neck. Do you feel it?" Lilly asked.

I placed my hand on the emulate that was around my neck. "I am in the attic, and I am here to rescue my family," I said as I opened my eyes. "Do you have the candle and stick?" I asked as soon as I saw her.

"Yes, I do. You were amazing," Lilly said.

"You are very talented, and did wonderful," she said.

"Now I need to make Sammy's hair into blood. But first, I need to cleanse this room of any evil. I need to restore the purity of the attic," Lilly said.

"Please hand me that sage stick, and grab one to help me," she said.

"We light these, and wave them all around in here. The smoke from it cleanses the air, so watch how I do it and then, you do it," Lilly said.

I watched how she did it, and I did the same. It smells like college memories I said remembering a time in college when I smoked pot.

"Yeah, it does smell like that, but it doesn't do anything to you. It's not a drug, but a cleanser," Lilly said. "All we need to do is get just outside the door, and we are ready to begin."

I went to the door, and cleansed it I guess. I wasn't sure how this stuff could do everything she said, but she was all I had right now and I needed her. "How are you going to turn that into blood?" I asked as I watched her mix some herbs with Sammy's hair.

"It is very difficult to do, but when you mix certain herbs and potions, with the fibers of someone, you can turn that into their blood. It can also be used to save the life of a mortal who has lost too much blood, but I wouldn't recommend offering it up at hospital, you might get committed," Lilly said with a laugh.

"I can see that," I said laughing at her joke about the hospitals. I watched very intently. She was right, it could be done. I watched as it began to turn into what looked like blood. "How do you know this will work?" I asked.

"I don't. But we only have one chance at making this work," she said.

"What happens if I mix it with my own blood?" I asked remembering a movie I watched where two girls cut their palms, and pressed them together and were blood sisters.

"You know I never thought of that, but it would work. You would be the next blood heir," she said thinking about it a minute. "We are going to put a little bit in this vile, and you must guard it with your life. If this doesn't work, we will mix it with your blood and make you a blood relative," Lilly said skeptically. "I have never done that before, and I really don't want to try it, but it is a good last resort," she said.

"Now what do we do?" I asked hoping she would tell me "Do we put the blood on the stick?" I asked.

"Not yet. I must read a little more to find out how to proceed," Lilly said. "Do you think you can concentrate really hard and see if you can see Trish and Sammy? I want to get them out first. They have been trapped longer than your husband and child," Lilly said.

"I can try," I said as I closed my eyes. Trish, I thought heavily. Breathing in and out slowly, I asked myself, 'Where were we when I last saw her?' We were in the living room, holding on to a chair or something, Trish please show yourself to me, I pleaded inside myself. Trish find me, I said to myself.

"There she is!" I cried. "She is stuck inside the wall of the living room, the far one, near the door."

"Good. Now try Sammy. Think really hard," Lilly said.

"Sammy is right there with her," I cried as I watched them both in the wall, having no idea what was happening. Seth and Jack are there too. Oh my baby. Mommy is coming. Please hold on baby, please!" I cried. I bawled. I couldn't help it. I wanted to be with my boys. They needed me.

"Natasha! Stop right now. You have to be strong. If you get stuck here, there is never going to be a way out," Lilly cried. "Natasha, follow my voice," Lilly said.

"Lilly, I have to get my boys," I screamed as the tears flowed down my face. "I will do anything, but I need them," I said.

"Natasha, we will get them. Now that we know the living room is the holding place, it is where the most magic is at. The curse is most powerful inside those walls," Lilly advised.

"What does that mean?" I asked confused by it all. "Can't I just focus on them and grab them like I did the candle and stick?" I asked.

"No, you can't. If you do, you risk getting sucked in. The force is stronger than anything you have ever came in contact with," Lilly warned. "We need to reboot our magic, and strengthen our souls before we enter that living room," she said.

"Ok, how?" I asked. I was willing to do anything at this point just to get them back. "Do I have to drink more nasty tasting potions? Bring them on. Do I need to power up with devil? Bring him on. I want my family back now!" I demanded. I couldn't help but feel this overwhelming anger and power surge through my body. "Natasha, I really don't think you need to reboot, but drink this. It will kick in when you need it,"

Lilly said handing me another potion. "It is going to taste nasty, but it works," she said.

I figured it would and drank it in one swallow. "You're right, it's gross. But hey, if it works it's worth it," I said.

"Natasha, once we enter the living room, the house is going to try and play with our minds. It will use your family- don't fall for it. Can you do that?" Lilly asked.

"I will try, but I can't promise," I said. "Is there a way to know if it's real rather than fake?" I asked hoping maybe it would help me differentiate the two.

"Yes, talk to them. If they don't respond in anyway, they're fake, but if they can communicate with you, then they are real," Lilly said.

"It sounds easy enough," I said feeling more confident about it.

"No it is not easy. You have to be able accept the fact that they are false, and not real. When you see Jack or Seth, you need to be stronger than the curse to bring them home," Lilly said.

"I know it will be hard, but if it's the only way to bring them home, then I will," I said. '*How can I look at a man who is my husband and child who I carried for nine months, and know they are just a figment of imagination?*' I wondered. I had to if I wanted to bring them home. Just keep telling yourself that, I said to myself.

"Natasha, we need to get to that living room. It is our only way to free them, and put an end to the curse," Lilly said. "Come on, you keep that emulate around your neck at all times, do you understand me?" Lilly ordered.

"Yes, I understand. It will not leave my neck," I said. I didn't understand how a simple necklace with a stone on it, could keep evil away, but I have never seen a house trap people, and do half the things this house has done, so I had to believe there was some magic around.

CHAPTER 12

The Power of the Curse

"Are we going to walk downstairs or are we going use magic to appear there?" I asked. "I'm not sure what would be worse … the anticipation of walking down the stairs and wondering what is going to happen, or just appearing inside the room that curse is most powerful, and has the most control."

"We are going to appear in the kitchen first, I need look around first. I don't want to be caught off guard by something I wasn't expecting," Lilly said. "There are certain herbs, I might need, and if they are in the kitchen, I can use them. But if they are not, then I need to use my back up plan."

"You have a lot plans. How do you know so much about this curse?" I asked. I was starting to wonder if she really was here to help us, or the curse. *I wish Trish was here. She would know what to do. She was always the one to come bail Ivy and me out of our problems, she was the strong one, I thought. Now I need to be the strong one who gets us out of here*, I thought to myself, more as a demand than a thought.

"Close your eyes, and think hard about the kitchen," Lilly ordered. I was becoming annoyed by her orders. It was just drink this, do this-but what choice did I have?

I closed my eyes and thought heavily on the kitchen. The kitchen was just on the other side of the living room. They shared a wall. I opened my eyes, and we were sitting in the kitchen, and Lilly was rummaging through the spices. "How did you get here so fast?" I asked realizing it looked like she had been in the kitchen long before me.

"I didn't. I just thought about the spice cupboard in the kitchen, so I had an advantage when I got in here," Lilly said.

"Sorry. It just caught me by surprise, when I opened my eyes and you were already in the cupboards," I said hoping it didn't sound like I was questioning her. I couldn't help but be leery of everything right now. This curse was so unpredictable I wasn't sure what was real and was fake any more.

"The herbs I need are here. Take this rosemary, and sprinkle it all over yourself and the kitchen. It provides protection, and any extra help is good," she said sincerely.

I took the rosemary and sprinkled it all around the kitchen and practically bathed in it myself. "I think it's good," I said laughing at how silly that must sound.

"This really isn't a laughing matter," Lilly said. "Now let's go into the living room and get set up."

"What do we need to get set up?" I asked. I guess I didn't realize we needed to prepare for this in some way. I thought we just went in and did it, and it was done.

"Well we need to put the blood on the stick, and candle so we can light at the right moment, and then we need set some traps, so when we see your family we can grab them and pull them back to reality," she said.

"I thought once we put the blood on the stick and lit the candle, they would be free," I said. I was very confused by this.

"Yes, the curse will be weakened and fragile, but the only way to get your family is to pull them into reality, and once their souls are released, the curse will be dead," she said. "Do you know how many other souls are trapped inside the walls of this house?" Lilly asked.

"No. I think it's just the grandfather, and my family, and friends," I said trying to remember. "How do we rescue others that have been here for years?" I asked.

"I am hoping that once we release your family, it will release past forgotten souls," Lilly said.

"You are hoping? What do you mean? You're not sure this is going to work?" I asked. "I thought you knew what you were doing," I stated. I could not believe she chose now to tell me she wasn't sure.

"I told you in the very beginning that there was a chance it would end badly so please, don't get upset with me because you wouldn't listen," Lilly snapped. "If we work fast, and accurate it should work, but we need the strength of a hundred Vikings, and the powers of Zeus, and the other guardians. If it's going to be just the two of us, please just do what I say," Lilly demanded.

"I'm sorry. I just want my family and friends back," I said with my head lowered. I understood why she was frigid, but I needed reassurance from her about this. I doubt she can give it to me though, I thought.

"Now, I need you angry," Lilly said. "Get mad, madder than you have ever been," she ordered. "If you are weakened by sorrow, or anything you have no chance. The curse will feed off that," she said. "Are you mad? Can you see colors other than red and black?" she asked. "Feel the rage. The curse stole your friends, and family. That beautiful little boy and the man you love were taken by the curse. Your soul mate was ripped from your world and your three best friends were consumed by the house. And now, the house is playing with your mind. It lets you get just close enough to see them and barely touch them, just before it rips them away, she persisted. Now let that rage, and anger over power you. Go with it," she said.

I was angry, I felt that the world owed me this; I wanted to see this house in flames, burning to ground, taking the curse to hell. I am angry, "I see red and only red," I said. "Let's get my family," I said standing up tall and firm. I felt a rage inside me that was more powerful than anything I had ever felt before. *I am going to shred this curse piece by piece*, I thought.

"Good," she said. "We are ready. Now we need to go in the living room and destroy the curse at its heart," Lilly said as if we were warriors in a war. "Come on, follow me," she said as she went to the door, looked over her shoulder and slid quietly through the door. I was right behind her.

"Ok, now we need to put the candle in the center of the room. It would be the heart of the curse," Lilly said. "Once we have it there we drop the blood on it and the stick then light the stick, then the candle. Got it?"

"Yes," I said. "I got a text from the house," I said as panic began to come to me.

"Ignore it. Do not open it. As a matter of fact, give it to me," she said, and threw it across the room. "There now, we don't have any idea of the games that are going to be played. All that those text messages were for was to keep you guessing and worrying. You don't need anything else to distract you from what we are doing," she said. "Are you ok?" she asked.

"Yeah, I am still mad, and I am actually happy about ending the guessing games," I said. "I just want to do what we have to and put an end to this," I said.

"Good. Now hand me the candle and stick," she said. "I am just going to do it. No questions and no second guessing," she said as she put drops of blood on the stick, and the candle. "I need those matches," she said holding her hand out.

I reached in my bag and looked for the matches, "I don't have them," I said surprised that they were no longer in my bag.

"What? I told you to grab them," she snapped. "Never mind, I will light it myself," she said as she lightly blew on it. It began to smoke and then a flame was on it. It was amazing. I had never seen anyone do anything like that before.

I watched as she placed the lit stick on the candle wick. Both were saturated with blood and they both lit up with a flame that sparked and shot out. The snapping and crackling sounds were not like normal candle sparks.

"Now, we need to focus on your friends and family so they will appear to us, and we can try and grab them. First we will focus on Sammy since she has been in the longest," Lilly said completely absorbed in this. "Focus on Sammy now. We must do it together," she ordered.

"Sammy, come to me, please. Sammy show yourself to me, please," I pleaded in my mind. "There she is!" I said as I opened my eyes. "Sammy, reach for me," I cried. "Please" I said as I reached out to grab her hand. I cried as my hand came in contact with hers. "Lilly help me," I cried as Lilly came rushing over to me.

"Pull Natasha, pull. If we work as one we can do it," she cried. "Evil, let go, evil give her back," Lilly chanted as we struggled to free her from the alternate world, the curse had created inside the walls of this house.

"Natasha," Sammy muttered. "Is that you? Please help me," she cried in a faint voice.

"I've got you Sammy. Fight the curse. Push through it," I cried as we both pulled and tugged on her. It felt like hours of pulling, and finally she came literally flying out and hit the floor. "Oh Sammy," I cried as I hugged her, so happy to see her.

"Sammy to the attic," Lilly said as she pointed her finger and Sammy disappeared. "She needs to be out of this room," Lilly said as I gave her a look of shock. "If she is in here, she is vulnerable to be captured again," Lilly said to reassure me of her actions.

"Now think of Trish. Bring Trish to the surface," she ordered. "Do it just as you did before. You have a stronger connection to them than me, so it is easier for you to connect," she said.

"Trish, please come to be please show yourself, let me save you. Please Trish," I pleaded. "Trish, I need you. Please Trish," I cried. "There she is!" I cried as I opened my eyes again. "Trish," I screamed as I reached out for her. "Grab my hand. Reach out. I won't let you fall," I cried as I got closer to her. "Trish, come on reach for me," I screamed as I touched her hand.

"Natasha, help me," she cried in a weak voice. "Please help me," she cried as I pulled on her.

"Natasha, keep pulling!" Demand the curse free her. Overpower the forces of evil that are holding her," Lilly demanded as she came up. "Trish, reach out and we will catch you," Lilly cried.

'Ouch,' Trish said as she hit the floor hard. 'Natasha,' she cried as she hugged me. 'I have you now,' she whispered in a deathly tone.

"What?" "Lilly it's not Trish," I screamed as I struggled to get her off me. "It's the curse. It is trying to take me," I cried as I finally pushed what looked like Trish off of me.

"Evil hath no entry here. Evil go back." Lilly chanted as she held up her stone and approached her. "Go back, back to your home, leave us," she ordered.

It was working, I watched as the curse or whatever it was back up into the wall and disappeared. "Now what do we do?" I cried realizing that curse was far more powerful than either of us had thought.

"We continue to get your friends and family," Lilly said. Now think of "Trish again, but think of her as she was when you last talked to her, like on the ride up here," Lilly said.

"Trish, remember your soon-to-be husband and your children. Trish, come on. I know you're here. Please come out, please," I begged as I opened my eyes.

"Natasha, help me. I have her but I can't pull her out alone. Please grab her other arm," Lilly screamed as she struggled to pull Trish.

"Trish, push past it. Come on, you can do it," I said as I pulled on her arm, struggling to free her. "Come back. You have two babies and a wonderful man to go home to. Fight this. Come back," I ordered as we pulled for all we were worth, and she too came flying out hitting the floor. "Trish, when did we meet," I asked before hugging her.

"Umm, we have been friends ever since we were kids. We grew up together. I don't remember the year. Your favorite color is camouflage, and you love trucks," she said laughing.

"OK, Trish I missed you," I said hugging her. It was great to have her back I thought.

"Trish to the attic," Lilly said as she pointed her finger again and Trish disappeared. "I know it's hard, but it needs to be done," she said. "Now think of Jack and Seth. Maybe we can pull them together," she ordered.

"My boys, I need you. Come back to me," I cried to them. "Please Seth, bring me my baby," I ordered as if he were in front of me. 'Please be there when I open my eyes,' I cried to myself and opened my eyes. "Seth!" I cried as he was standing there in front of me, holding my baby boy.

"Wait! What is her middle name," Lilly demanded before I could run to them. Natasha, remember-we have to be sure. One mistake can send you into the walls of the curse," Lilly said.

"What is our dog's name?" I asked. "What do you call my parents?" I demanded.

"Our dogs name is Sparky," Seth said "and your middle name is Rain. It is one of the main reasons I love you, you're unique."

"He's right," I said. Jack what do you call your parents?" I ordered before they stepped a foot closer.

"Mommy, I call them Mema, and Pepa" Jack said just as he always does. "Why am I in trouble? I was a good boy while you were gone" Jack asked with tears in his eyes.

"Oh baby you're not, I love you" I said, as I kissed them both.

"To the attic," Lilly said as she pointed and they were gone. "I know it's hard, but we are almost done, Ivy needs us, then we can be together," she said.

"Ivy, damn you, you ignorant girl show yourself," I ordered. "I know you can hear me, I cried. Please don't make me lose you. Come on please Ivy," I cried. "Damn it Ivy, get your stubborn ass out here now," I screamed as I opened my eyes. I cried as she too was standing in the doorway. "What did we get drunk on for the first time?" I asked.

"Easy, Tequila Rose. We drank the entire fifth before going to a rodeo." she said laughing. "Get over here and hug me," she ordered.

"I ran to her. She was the only one who knew that. I knew it was her, I thought. "Ivy to the attic," I said and pointed my finger, and she disappeared.

"Good. Now we free the curse," Lilly said. "We must put the book back in the rightful hands."

"How are we going to do that?" I asked. "If it happened many years ago, centuries ago, how are we going to give it back to her?"

"You are going to visit the past. Close your eyes, and think of the guardian of all good magic. You must focus intently on her," Lilly said.

I closed my eyes, thinking of all that is good, and the creator of good magic.

"Do you see anything?" Lilly asked. "Remember to keep your focus, tell me what you see, any little bit of detail to bring your focus closer," she said as I tried to remember anything from the book.

Deep breaths in and out, I told myself. There are people in ragged dresses, and clothes. It looks to be 1800's. No vehicles-just horses, and wagons," I said as I watched them scurrying about. I see a woman who is carrying a sag type bag. It has stones, like the ones on our necklaces," I said as I watched this woman walking around like she was searching for something. There is a woman who is wandering about like she is searching for something. I am looking for something that says her name, but I don't seem to see anything," I said.

"Are there people near her that could call her by name?" Lilly asked. "Stay focused, and ask someone nearby to call her by name," Lilly said. "It will be easy. Just think it really hard and they will oblige you," she said. "Just be very careful that you don't lock hands with them. They can pull you in," Lilly warned.

Nothing like more pressure, I thought. I concentrated intently on the person who was nearest to the woman, call her by name, I thought.

"Excuse me Glory," the man said. "Can I help you find something?"

"Glory," I called to draw her attention to me, instead of that man. "I have something that belongs to you," I said as she began to approach me.

"Do I know you?" she asked as she looked at me with a very strange expression.

"No. I am sorry to bother you, but I believe these are yours," I said holding up the book, and candle. "It is a very long story, but I have been trapped in this curse for a day or so and I must be giving you back your book. It belongs to you," I said as I lightly handed it to her.

"Thank you. But I didn't know it was missing," she said.

Oh that's right, this is the past, I thought. "It is not missing yet, but a man stole it from you and you cursed the man and his family until it was returned to you, and good magic was protected again," I said trying to avoid any contact with her. "Please take the book, and end the curse, I am begging you."

"Of course, I will be happy to. I am not sure how or what has happened, but I will be sure to keep this secure, and free you of any harm," she said as she lifted the book from my hands.

"Thank you, but it is time for me to return to my home, and time," I said with a laugh. "You see I am from a time in the future-the two thousands. Thank you again," I said and focused on my time, the house and Lilly.

"Are you back?" I heard Lilly ask. "Careful, don't push past it. You must transit slowly so nothing has been changed," she warned.

"Yes, I am back, and I am glad to be back," I said as I opened my eyes. "Is the curse over? Can we all go home? I asked. "Can I see my family?" I begged.

"Of course. Attic!" she said as she snapped her fingers and we were standing in the attic, with Trish, Sammy, Ivy and my boys.

"Oh I missed you," I cried as I hugged Seth and Jack first. "Are you guys alright?" I asked as the tears began to fall from eyes.

"Do I even want to know what happened this weekend?" Seth asked as he kissed me.

"No. But I will tell you after we leave," I said still hugging my boys. "Are you alright Trish and Sammy?" I asked as I hugged them too. Sammy seemed different; her hug wasn't the same as before.

"Yes we are fine, Sammy said in a strange tone. Can we go home now?" she asked.

"Yes, let's all go home," I said and snapped my fingers. We were all standing outside next to the vehicle, it was a wonderful site. "Can I burn the house down now?" I asked as a joke.

"No it will serve no purpose. The curse is gone," Lilly said. "Keep the house here as a reminder of your strength, and everything you have overcome," Lilly said smiling.

CHAPTER 13

Danger Among Us

"Let's all meet back at my house, and have some dinner and celebrate," I said smiling. I was thankful to be out of this nightmare. "We deserve it after everything we've been through this weekend."

"Yes, that is a great idea," Sammy said. She was beginning to act more like herself, it was nice to see her, but I wasn't sure how to mention her being pregnant. "Who wants to drive? I really don't feel like it," she said laughing.

"We don't need to," Lilly said. "Everyone get in the car, and Natasha, Ivy and I will show you how we put an end to the curse," Lilly said giving me a look of pride.

We all piled into the jeep yet again, but this time we were going home. Seth was seriously glued to me. His hand never left mine. It was nice to be in his arms again, I thought. "Ok, everyone," I said as the three of us closed our eyes, and snapped our fingers.

"Hey we are home" Seth said when we opened our eyes. "How did you do that?" he asked very confused, and excited.

"It was Lilly. She gave us some herbal medicine to help us bring you guys home, and one of the side effects is mystical powers for three days," I said laughing. "Come on lets go inside," as I opened my door and got out.

"Natasha is there any way you guys could get my babies here," Trish asked. I could tell she really wanted her babies to be with her.

"Go inside. There is a surprise waiting for you," I said. The look on her face was priceless. She wasn't sure what I had done, but when everyone else was thinking about home-I thought about the loved ones who weren't here, and brought them here for the girls.

"Oh my goodness," I heard Trish scream from the house. "Natasha, how did you...?" she started to say as she ran up to me, and hugged me. "Thank you so much," she said still hugging me. "Guys, I want you to meet Scott, he is my fiancé," she said as he walked up next to her.

He was very cute, and he looked at her with undeniable love in his eyes. "Hi Scott," I said as I shook his hand. "It's great to meet you."

"I have heard so much about all of you, I feel like we have been friends forever," he said laughing.

"Sammy what is wrong?" I asked, as I noticed her scowling look. "Are you feeling alright?"

"Yeah, I am just a little tired, I guess. I haven't been feeling like myself lately," she said. "Is it alright if I go lay down?" she asked.

"Of course honey. Please, go on in and rest," I said, maybe with a little too much concern in my voice.

"Is she alright?" Trish asked "Is she hurt, or something?" She was unable to cover her concern.

"Sammy, have you missed a period lately?" Ivy bluntly asked "How about weird cravings, anything unusual?"

"Why?" Sammy asked very defensively "Well, I haven't had a period in a couple months, but I have been under a great deal of stress at work," Sammy said still sounding very confused.

"You're pregnant," Ivy blurted right out.

"Ivy, you couldn't have told her any other way?" I snapped "That was just flat out insensitive," I said glaring at her.

"What are you guys talking about?" Sammy asked with a look of shock on her face.

"Let's all go inside and we can talk," I suggested and began walking towards the house. "Come on," I said as I looked back. They followed me, all looking very uneasy about the situation. "Please guys have a seat. I will start the coffee, and we can talk," I said.

"No. Let me make coffee, and you girls talk. There is obviously something going on," Seth said. "Scott and I will talk and watch the children," he said as looked at Scott who seemed very frightened by the sight of us talking.

"Thank you dear," I said kissing him, and hugging my little man again. I didn't want either of them out of my sight, but I knew I had to tell Sammy about the book and her pregnancy.

"Ok, Sammy. We looked at the family tree, and a book that was made completely by magic. It was updated magically as the world happened," I said. "Well, it said that you were the blood heir to the legacy, not Ivy" I said, watching her expression very closely. "You see once you got past the first stage of pregnancy, it told us that you were going to have this baby, and it was the heir," I continued.

"How can that be? Ivy is the blood relative," Trish asked, trying to make sense of this. "Are they sisters or something?"

"No we are not sisters," Sammy interrupted. "Ivy stole my family when she was a baby. It was me who was supposed to grow up rich and spoiled, not her," Sammy snapped glaring at Ivy. "You see, we share a birth date, and some stupid nurse got us mixed up when we were babies. That is why I'm the heir, not her," she said still glaring at Ivy.

"Sammy, I am sorry, that's not my fault," Ivy said with a shocking level of concern in her voice. "How did you find this out?" Ivy asked?

"After my parents died in horrible car crash, I became very depressed, and began looking through stuff. I came across our hospital documents, and it said that we were switched at birth, but our parents didn't want switch us back. They thought it would be best for live as we were," she said.

"Wait! Let's not get upset you guys. We have been through a huge dramatic event this weekend," I said trying to end the battle as I watched the burning in Sammy's eyes. "Sammy, I'm sorry about that, but you were both babies, and Ivy couldn't have known this then," I said.

"I don't really care if she did or she didn't. She has always acted better than all of us, and this weekend she was going to pay," Sammy said standing up. "I don't think she meant to tell us that." The evil in her eyes were undeniable.

"Sammy come on," Trish said trying to calm her. "Sammy, you and Ivy have been friends for a really long time. Please don't let this wreck your friendship," Trish said sweetly.

"Friendship? You have to be kidding me," Sammy said with a laugh.

"Wait just a minute, you nutcase," Ivy interrupted. "What do you mean, I was going to pay?" Ivy asked. You really think this is my fault. I was an infant, the same as you. How could I have known a nurse would switch us?" Ivy snapped.

I could see it in Ivy's eyes. She was ready to explode. Sammy was way off base and Ivy was going to let her have it.

"You were going to get just what you deserved this weekend. I had it all planned out. There was going to be a terrible accident on the slopes that left you in coma, or paralyzed," Sammy said with the look of death in her eyes.

I looked to Lilly for some type of help. Maybe she could bind them to their chairs or anything to keep this from turning deadly. Lilly just looked at me with a look of remorse, like she knew it would end badly.

"Enough, you two, I stood up and said. Get a hold of yourselves. You are acting like idiots," I snapped. "I for one am happy as hell to be home with my family again, and you Sammy have a baby on the way, so get used to it. Ivy you are married. Maybe your husband would like to know you are home," I snapped, I had reached my boiling point, and I knew Trish was right there behind me.

"A baby is on the way and do you want to know who the father is?" Sammy snapped "It's Lance, your husband. We have been screwing each other for about six months, and he knew of my plan this weekend. He was a part of it. It was the only way we could get our money," she snapped.

"You have crossed the line now," Ivy said and lunged for her. "Baby or no baby you have gone too far."

"Stop it you two," Trish screamed. She hated drama, and after this weekend I don't think she could take anymore. "Please" she cried.

"Lilly, help me," I cried as I closed my eyes and tried to think of place to go. As I opened my eyes, I was standing in a hospital nursery. I looked down there were two baby girls. They were Ivy and Sammy. *Why am I here* I wondered? "Was I supposed to switch them back or something?"

"No Natasha, you are not. You will forever change the course of everyone's life around you," Lilly said as she stood next to me. "You are here to learn. They are babies right now and they don't know you. But, for some reason you came back to the beginning where it all began," she continued to tell me.

"If I can't fix it, then why I am here?" I asked. I was beyond confused.

"Look at their parents watching them. They love those baby girls. They think each is theirs. Now imagine if you were asked, a few years down the road to give that beautiful baby to another woman," Lilly said. Now, hold my hand. We are going back and you are going to show them this," Lilly ordered.

I opened my eyes again I was standing in my living room. There was Ivy and Sammy fighting on the floor, just as when I left. I reached down and grabbed them, closed my eyes, and brought them back to what I had just witnessed.

"How did we get here?" Sammy asked.

"If you two would stop your fighting, and look at what is in front of you, I will tell you," I said firmly. "We are at the hospital where you were born, on the day you were born. Look at your parents," I ordered. "They look so happy staring at you two in the nursery," I said making them realize how much their parents loved them. "Do you see it?" I demanded.

"Yeah, my mother was so beautiful. I was all she ever wanted," Sammy said as she watched her mother, remembering how special she was.

"Yeah, mine too" Ivy said in a voice of shock. "My mother looks like she has just been giving the most important thing to her" she said still starring at her.

"Yeah. Now, how do you think they felt when they were asked to give you away to a woman they didn't know, knowing they would never see you again?" I snapped. "Do you think they thought, well maybe I could give her away? Who cares if she is with a family who doesn't love her as much as I do?" "Yeah it was hard to say no after learning the truth, but in their heart you were their child no one else's." I said sweetly hoping they would understand. "Now do you understand Sammy? It wasn't Ivy who did it, it was your mother," I snapped at her for being so ignorant to the matter.

"Yeah, I guess I do," she said in a flat tone of zero emotion. "Can we go home now?" she asked.

"Just a minute," Ivy said. "Can they see us?" Ivy asked "I really want to go to the waiting room for just a moment to see if my, I mean our grandfather is there," she said.

"No, they can't see us," I said smiling. It made me happy to see them see the reality of the matter. "Can we come?" I asked, curious to see her grandfather, the man who helped us get out of the curse with his journals.

"I would like to stay here and just watch my mother," Sammy said starring at her mom.

"Ok, we will be right back," Ivy said as we began to walk to the waiting room. "Do you think he is there?" Ivy asked. She was very curious about her grandfather. All the memories she had of him were from so long ago, and not many at that.

"I think so," I said as we poked our heads to see if he was there.

He was. He was there talking to the other people, waiting for the news of their new family members. He looked so happy.

"Wow, he looks so much younger than I remember," Ivy said smiling. "Ok, we can go now. I just needed to see if he was as happy about me, and he was," she said.

As we walked back to Sammy, I noticed a strange look on her face, but I couldn't put my finger on it. She looked satisfied or something-like she got her way. "Sammy, are you ready?" I asked starring at her for some emotion.

"Yeah, I am ready. It was nice to see my mother and father, but it just reminded me of how much I miss them," she said.

"Home," I said and snapped my fingers. I opened my eyes, and we were not in my living room. I was completely alone, and in a very large apartment. "*Where am I?*" asked looking around for someone to answer me. "Seth, Jack!" I cried as I walked through the rooms. This place is amazing, I thought-but where am I? Where was my family? "Lilly," I screamed hoping she was there, and could answer this for me?

"Yeah," a voice said.

"Lilly is that you?" I cried?

"Yes, it is. But in this place, I am not Lilly. I am Lila, a street performer," she said.

"How....I didn't do anything," I cried. "Where is my family?" I cried, "Please tell me. I just got them back. Don't tell me, I lost them again," I said as the tears streamed down my face?

"Sammy switched the babies back, while you and Ivy went to see her grandfather, and it changed everything," she said. "You never got pregnant with Seth. You spent all your college years studying and getting all A's, and you have a great job working in advertising."

"What? I am not a writer? I don't have Jack? Those are the things that make me, me. How can they not be?" I asked completely puzzled. "What about Seth?"

"You never met. You got a great job right out of school, and had scholarships, so you never had to pay for a thing. You never bartended, and that is where you met Seth," Lilly said pointing out the obvious changes in my life, and Seth's.

"What about Trish, I asked hoping I didn't screw her world up too?" I asked still afraid of what she might say.

"Trish is still your friend, but her life has changed as well. She is not getting married. She has two children. On the plus side, she is richer than belief. She married a very old man, who left her his entire will, so she has nannies, and servants to care for her kids now," she said.

I couldn't help the tears as they began to flow, they world was gone and everything I had ever known was gone. "I want my life back," I cried. "Help me, please."

"I can, but it won't be easy. We have to go back to the hospital where it all began and change them back, but that will be on you. Sammy will probably hate you forever," Lilly said.

"I don't care. I want my-our lives back," I said.

She closed her eyes, snapped her fingers, and there I was standing with Sammy and Ivy.

I knelt down and carefully switched the names back to how they were. I couldn't risk losing everything we had all worked so hard at getting. Even Sammy, who had a great career and Ivy, who had spent most of her time partying and picking up men, but it was them ... they earned that. I closed my eyes, and said "home."

As I opened my eyes, I saw Trish sitting in the chair, looking completely beside herself, while Sammy and Ivy screamed at each other. Sammy, you have got to be the most ungrateful, despiteful, evil person I have ever meant. I screamed and grabbed Sammy, knocking her to the ground. "Just because you had to deal with the loss of your parents, and not being rich, you want to destroy our lives," I screamed.

"What are you talking about?" she snapped "I haven't done anything. It was all Ivy's fault," she screamed and lunged at Ivy again. "Ivy is the one who has lived the life of a rich little snob her whole life, when it was supposed to me. I was the one who was supposed to have the life of luxury, not her," Sammy cried.

"Sammy, listen to yourself," I cried. "You are blaming her for something your parents did to you. It was your mother who chose you over her, not the other way around," I said, completely dumbfounded by her. "Sammy, you are the one who tried to destroy our lives. You switched the babies, when we weren't looking-so that makes you the monster not her," I snapped hoping she would realize how ignorant she was being.

"Alright," Seth burst in and said, "I have kept quiet long enough but this is an outrage. You three are acting like idiots, and I am done," he screamed loud enough to be heard.

"Yeah," Scott said, agreeing with Seth. "Why are you guys spending this time fighting, when you should really be thinking how good it is to be alive? You were all almost killed this weekend, and your families were in danger as well. And you three are fighting with each other over what?" Scott announced.

"He is right," I said calmly. "We need to be celebrating our life, not fighting the ones we have," I said placing my hand on Sammy's arm.

I never saw it coming, but Sammy swung around and struck me hard across the face, as if it were I who had hurt her. "You are so stupid Natasha. How can you be so naïve? You think your life is so perfect. You got the perfect man, the greatest kid, but guess what?" Sammy sneered. "Your wonderful husband had an affair," she blurted out.

"No, you are lying," I said. "You are just trying to make me question my life, because you are so unhappy with yours."

"No, it's true. Ask Trish. She is the one who told me. She witnessed him, and some red headed slut, checking into the Plaza, when he was supposed to be away on business a few months ago. Go on Trish tell her," Sammy cried.

"Trish, is this true?" I asked looking to her and then to Seth, who looked like he just got caught stealing cookies from the cookie jar. "Don't answer. I can tell it is true by the look in his eyes," I said looking directly into his eyes.

"So, you want to tell me everything is how it should be?" Sammy asked starring into my soul, as her eyes burned through my exterior.

"Actually Sammy, yes I do. I don't care if Seth had affair, which will be handled on our time, not in front of anyone else," I said glaring at her. "Also, if this is the type of person you are, then you deserve all the heart ache and misery you've got," I snapped. "Now if you will excuse yourself, you can leave. The door is in the same place it was when you came in," I said. "I do not wish to have you in my home anymore, and I hope you are happy. Your mission is accomplished," I said as I turned to walk away.

"Don't you walk away from me Natasha. You are not in control. This is my game now," Sammy said as she walked quietly up behind me.

"NO, you are wrong," I said as I spun around and nailed her right in the mouth with my fist. "This is not a game. This is life, and you have managed to turn a celebration of life into a separation of life," I said standing my ground.

Sammy looked completed stunned by the reaction she got from me. I was not a violent person, never had been, but she crossed the line and knew it.

"Natasha, I am so sorry," Trish said coming up to me. "I know I should have told you, but you were so happy, and I didn't have the heart to break yours," Trish said as the tears streamed down her cheeks.

"Trish, I know. I am not mad at you, but you should have told me," I said hugging her. It was a hard situation to be in, I said looking at Seth.

I looked at Sammy, closed my eyes and said, "The house of never ending," and snapped my fingers. When I opened my eyes she was standing there in front of me. What! "Why didn't that work?" I said looking at Lilly who was just sitting quietly.

"Natasha you can't use your magic for revenge or evil. If you do, you will be forever cursed and live a life of evil," Lilly said walking up to me. "I stopped it from working, but if you choose to do it again, knowing the consequences, I will not stop it. So, ask yourself if it's worth it before you sentence a young girl who is or was a best friend to a life of hell."

"No, it's not. Thank you, I am sorry. I shouldn't have tried to use magic to solve this problem. I need to act like an adult and settle this woman to woman," I said looking eagerly at Sammy.

"Now Sammy, do you want to settle this with me or Ivy? But whoever you choose, it is the end of this battle, no more baby mix up, or affair; nothing," I said staring at her. "Remember, we are all friends here, and I am not going to stop living my life because you can't get one of your own, and you are stuck playing second to everyone's man," I said looking at her. The question is, were you the red headed slut, Trish saw Seth with?" I asked.

"Actually yes it was me."

"I thought so," I said completely calm, no emotion or anything in my face. "Who is it going to be, Sammy? Are you going to pick me, or Ivy the one who has had special treatment her whole life, and taken many classes in martial arts?" I asked, hoping it was me.

"You," Sammy said. "You married Seth, and I loved him from the moment we met. And he loves me to," she said. "He is actually the father of my baby," she said holding her stomach, like it was going to help her.

"Well, if all your drinking this weekend, and scams hasn't hurt the baby then, I am sure, just hitting your lying, cheating face won't either," I said as I drew my fist back and struck her in the mouth again.

"Ahh," she screamed and lunged at me. We wrestled and swung at each other, barely connecting, yelling at each other.

"Enough, Seth said as he grabbed us, pulling us apart. Stop this," he cried. "She is with child-with my child," he cried.

I stopped dead in my tracks, realizing that one of my best friends was pregnant with my husband's child. "You're right Seth, this is craziness," I said and smacked him hard as I could, putting my whole body, my whole broken heart into that hit, sending him to the floor. "You can leave now," I cried and threw my ring at his face, hitting him in the eye. "I am done, Seth. Take your trash and get out," I screamed pushing Sammy at him. "Enjoy your new family, but I am warning you she is crazy," I said and picked up Jack who had watched that whole ordeal, and walked out.

"Natasha, stop please." Seth came running behind me. "Please let me explain," he begged. I could tell he felt terrible about it, and was truly sorry.

"Seth, what are you wasting your time for? You got what we planned. We are together now and she can't come between us anymore," Sammy yelled following behind him.

"Sammy, go to hell," Trish said and shoved her, sending her directly down 15 steps approximately. "Oh no!" Trish cried as Sammy hit the landing of the stairs, she realized what had just happened.

Both Seth and I spun around to see what the commotion was about. "Call 911," I yelled as I stared at Sammy lying there unconscious at the bottom of the stairs. "Do it!" I screamed as I saw Seth, frozen by the sight of her.

"Natasha, come here, and form a circle with everyone now," Lilly ordered. We all formed the circle. She closed her eyes, and said "hospital." We opened our eyes in a blink and we were at the hospital.

"Seth, go check her in," I snapped at him. He ran to the front desk. "Trish, can you please take Jack to the waiting room or cafeteria?" I asked handing her my wallet. I walked up to Seth, and I heard him say, "It's my girlfriend. She fell down the stairs, and she is pregnant," I couldn't say anything. I just stared at him.

The nurses lifted her on to a gurney and took her in a room. I followed, but I wasn't sure if I was relieved that she was hurt, after what she had done, or if I was scared. I was angry with Seth for betraying our love, breaking our vows and breaking my heart, but she was one of my best friends. Do I write them both off, or fix it? I sat there wondering, and staring off into space.

"Natasha, Natasha," Seth said trying to bring me back to reality. "Hey, she is going to be alright, but she lost the baby," he said. It was hard to tell what he was feeling. He almost seemed happy about Sammy losing the baby.

I bowed my head. I couldn't look at him. "Go now, is all I can say to you," I said lifting my head a little. "I need to make sure she is alright," I said and went to her side.

"Natasha, I am your husband. Please talk to me," he begged.

"Yeah, you are my husband. What does that even mean?" I said looking into his eyes, and seeing the pain he had. "I may be your wife, but I am not yours right now. You chose to sleep with my friend and get her pregnant, so now I have to comfort her, for the loss of her baby, when I am glad she lost it," I said sternly staring at the floor, ashamed of how I felt. "So please, forgive me for not giving two ounces for your feelings right now," I said and pushed him away.

"Natasha, what do you expect me to do? You are always busy-always on a deadline, and Jack is the only thing that you care about in our home," Seth cried. "Yes, I was wrong, but I was alone. I had no one there to comfort me, no one to take care of me, and she came over one day while you were on a book event and we talked. Then it turned into something a little more, and before I knew it she was bringing me cookies and drinks, and coming over when you were away. I never meant for that to happen, I never even saw it coming," he begged.

"Seth, go," I cried as a nurse walked in.

"Is everything alright?" the nurse asked.

"No, this man pushed her down the stairs," unaware that the words even came out of my mouth.

"Natasha, what did you just do?" Seth said as he looked at me. That is not true, Seth cried as the nurse looked at him.

"Miss, are you sure?" the nurse asked me, I could tell she was looking for the truth.

"No, it is not true," I said and looked at the nurse. "You see, she is one of my best friends. She was in my wedding, and this is my husband. I just found out about their affair and then one thing lead to another. She came at me, I defended myself, and she fell down the stairs," I said lying to cover up Trish. But I didn't know she was pregnant, and I didn't mean for her to fall. I was defending myself," I said, hoping the nurse would have a soft spot in her heart for my broken heart. "I am sorry truly sorry for saying it was him, but as you can see, this is a very messy situation. We just survived a horrid weekend that nearly killed us, and then, when we finally got home, another secret was revealed. I think we are just very emotional, and that is why our dispute turned violent. I never meant for her to fall, or get hurt in any way. I was merely protecting myself," I said lowering my head in defeat.

"Alright. I am not going to report this only because I just found out my husband of twenty years, has had a girlfriend for ten of those years," the nurse said lowering head as well. "I know if given the chance, I would probable do a lot worse to the other woman in my case, but please don't tell anyone else of this, I could lose my job," she warned.

"Thank you. I am very sorry about your husband," I said knowing how she must feel; as cold as ice, and hard as stone.

"Natasha, will you please talk to me? I have to explain," Seth begged. "You know you and Jack are my world. There is nothing more important to me," he pleaded. "Natasha, we have been through so much together and we have always been able to talk it out. So please, just come out in the hallway and talk to me," he cried. I could tell his heart was breaking at the sight of mine turning to ice.

I was just about to say yes, and Sammy squeezed my hand. Sammy, I cried as felt her grip on my hand. "Are you awake? Please Sammy, open your eyes," I cried. "Nurse, come quick. She's waking up," I screamed.

"Natasha," she whispered. I leaned in closer to hear her. "I am sorry," she said.

"Sorry? Sweetie, I am sorry. But let's not talk about that right now. Let's just get you healthy," I said softly.

Trish poked her head in and said. "Excuse me Natasha, but I think you should come here."

"Ok, but this better be good"

"Natasha, that is not Sammy," Trish said pointing a girl sitting next Scott, who was identical to Sammy.

"What?" I said. I was completely shocked. "Who are you?" I asked.

"Natasha, it is me Sammy. That girl in there is not me, I met her a couple weeks ago, and I guess she is my sister-well twin, but I don't know all the facts yet. She came to me, and told me about mine and Ivy's true identities, and then the next thing I knew, you all hated me, and canceled this weekend," Sammy said.

"How do I know, you are telling me the truth?" I asked. I couldn't help but question her right now. This was just too crazy. "Tell me something only Sammy would know," I demanded.

"What do you want me to tell you? Jack weighed six pounds and point three ounces when he was born and you threw up the first time you told Seth you loved him," she said. "Natasha, Trish has filled me in on everything. I have a lot more sense than that to blame Ivy for something that happened when we were infants, and I would never sleep with Seth, nor would I try to hurt any of you, even Ivy. She might be a total snob, and stuck on herself, but you are all my sisters-even her," Sammy said.

"It is you!" I cried and hugged her. "That still doesn't answer Seth having an affair with her," I said puzzled.

"Natasha, get in here," Seth came out and yelled.

We all ran in there. "What is it?" I asked.

"You tell them the truth now," he ordered to that girl, who ever she is. "Please, you must. You have hurt us all so much as it is," he cried. "Don't let me lose my family, just like you lost yours, please!" he begged her.

"Seth, really?! … I am not in the mood to hear excuses about your affair," I snapped.

"No, listen" the girl said. He did have an affair, but it wasn't a willing one. I have been drugging him with this love potion. Lilly and I have been scamming you guys for months, and Seth never really cheated on you-he was drugged, and in about thirty six hours, everything will be out of his system. All he will remember is thinking it was all a dream until now," she said.

"Lilly? What does Lilly have to do with this?" I questioned.

"We set the whole thing up with the house, and the curse. We heard the house was haunted, and we purposely got your plans for this weekend. It was Lilly texting you all weekend," she said.

"No, Lilly saved us," I cried. "It can't be true," I said. "How you could do all this?" I asked.

"Magic. Both Lilly and I practice magic. We only used our powers for good, but then somehow we turned dark, and now we use it to steal mainly," she said. Her words were like daggers, something cruel and evil. "Please believe me, I am sorry. I never meant for this to happen, and I never meant to get pregnant. That was not part of our plan, but you need to know the truth," she said.

"Who are you?" I screamed. "Why us? What did you gain from this?" I cried. "How could you be so despicable? We have nothing of value to you, nor do we deserve this," I stated. I stood unyielding above her, as she lay there in the bed, staring helplessly up at me, begging for mercy in her eyes. "You are going to give me answers. I want the truth," I commanded.

"I will tell you anything you want to know," she said. "I promise, no more lies and games. I am done with it all," she cried. "I want to start making amends for past mistakes, and wrong doings. So please, let me start with you," she said as the tears flowed heavily down her cheeks.

"No, this is not going to be for your moral conscience-this is for us," I demanded. "How did you do this? How did you make the curse," I screamed. I couldn't help the emotions exploding from me. This woman, nearly killed us, and turned us against each other. "Better yet, start from the beginning. I want to know everything," I said, pulling up a chair next to her.

"Yeah. We deserve to know. You destroyed a happily married couple by drugging the man and getting pregnant. You turned two friends into enemies, and you made us think

Sammy was deceitful, and horrid," Trish cried as she too pulled up a chair, eagerly awaiting some answers.

"Yeah. We want answers too. You told Sammy and me that we have been living a life that isn't ours-that we were switched at birth and now you are going to tell us," Ivy demanded as she pulled a chair in close, fuming inside herself.

"Yeah, start talking," Sammy said. She was still very confused about everything, unsure of what happened.

"Seth, Scott, will you two please take the children home, get them some dinner and then just let them play? Conner and Darla can sleep in the spare room, or lay some sleeping bags out in the living room, and let them all have a slumber party out there," I stated, terrified by what we might find out. "They don't need to be here for this. Who knows how long it will take to get the truth?" I said shaking my head at that girl.

"Yeah, of course my love," Seth said leaning in to kiss me. "Please Natasha. You and Jack are my world. Please," he begged.

"Thank you Seth. I love you too," I reluctantly said and let him kiss me. It was more for him than me, I was far to confused to fight at this point. My heart bled from betrayal but cried tears of joy to know it wasn't his choice. I kissed Jack, I hated to leave him again, but we needed answers.

"Thank you, Scott," Trish said kissing him, and the kids. "We will be home as soon as we can," she said and hugged them again good bye.

CHAPTER 14

The Truth

"Excuse me," a short heavy, nurse came in and said. "She really needs some rest, so I am going to ask you all you to go home, and come back tomorrow," she said sternly.

"No, we are not leaving. This woman has been lying and betraying us for months. We are not leaving until, we get the truth," Ivy snapped. Ivy has never liked the word no, and she wasn't going to except right now.

"I am sorry miss, but you have to leave," the nurse said.

"It is alright, I want them here," the betrayer said as she titled the bed up to an upright position. "I am fine. They need to know," she said staring the nurse in the eyes.

"Alright. But I better not have to break up any fights. I am not a bouncer, so please don't make me be one," the nurse said, and walked away.

"Thank you. That was actually the right thing to do. How hard it must have been for you," I said smugly.

"Ok, first of all my name is Sarah," she said. "It all started back in June. Lilly and I had finished our internship at the hospital, she said. We found Sammy and Ivy's birth records, and the legal document signed by both parents and lawyers, stating that, 'the hospital had made a mistake, and switched the babies, but both parties involved were signing off any rights to the other child, and we're not going to pursue any legal action', and that got us thinking," Sarah said.

"How could that make you think?" I snapped.

"It made us think, that we could turn a profit off them," she said clearly irritated by my outburst. "We began doing some more intense research, and we found you, Natasha, a renowned author, famous for your romance and fiction words, and then we knew we could make some good cash. Your name is all over the internet, all over the book stores, everywhere," she continued. "So we began looking to Trish, your best friend and biggest supporter. You even dedicated one of your books to her," she said glaring at me.

"This doesn't make any sense," Ivy quipped.

"You wanted me to start from the beginning didn't you?" she asked. "After we gathered all your back grounds, and information, we came across some interesting news about the house and the curse. Thus, we came up with a plan," she said smiling at her words.

"Why are you smiling? This is not a funny story," Sammy said.

"Oh it gets better. You see with Natasha always busy, working on books, tours and book signings and her husband, poor poor Seth, was stuck in the shadows. But, he always seemed so proud and supportive of his dear wife, and that's when we decided to look more into Natasha's schedule. We found out that, once a month she was going to be away for about week. She always took Jack with her, but poor Seth had to work, so he couldn't partake of his wife's travels," she said smugly looking at me.

"You took advantage of a man who stood by his wife's side, and loved to do so," I snapped ... I was fuming ... I wanted to rip her head off those smug shoulders. My eyes must have had flames in them.

"Natasha, stop," Trish said to me. "She is trying to get under your skin. Calm down," she insisted.

"You're right," I said and relaxed a bit more.

"It was then that we conjured a lookalike spell on me, so I would look just like Sammy," she said smiling. "It was then that I decided to make my move on Seth. So I went to your home, when you were off doing your books, and doted on Seth. I kept going over there whenever you were gone. Each time, I gave him some of my homemade love spell, and ha, it only took two doses, and he was mine," she laughed.

I kept my mouth shut, trying to avoid strangling her. I just smiled.

"Once I knew he was mine, I started getting more subtle. Then one night I called him, pretending to be all upset and needing his comfort," she said laughing at her remembrance of that night. "He came running to me and I acted as if I was so distraught and hurt, he stayed all night holding me. Then with just a little dose, we made passionate love all night, and well, after that, it was easy. I kept giving him the drug, and he kept coming," she said obviously enjoying, the pain it brought me.

"You are pure Satan, aren't you?" Sammy cried. "How could you play him like that, and do it looking like me?" she said completely disgusted.

"You were the easy one. Always tied to your career, never in meaningful relationships and always wanting what they had," she said laughing at us. "That is when I decided to make my move on you Sammy. A few phony messages from them, and canceling the trip. You're so naïve and stupid, it was easy to throw you off the scent," she said.

"This is not making sense," Ivy said. "How did you get the house to be like that?" she asked trying to get the *story moving.*

"I will get to that" she said. "As it drew closer to your trip, Lilly worked day in and out, planning. She really is a master mind," Sarah said. "It was easy to get the house to be cursed, because it was already, a possessed property. All we needed to do was make it active, and we put a hex on it, so that once you were in, you couldn't get out. We knew that you guys would do the rest-give us all the back ground information trying to free your friends," she said, still laughing at how shocked we were.

"Ok, just so I am clear on this," Trish said. "You drugged Seth into sleeping with you, and tricked Sammy into thinking we didn't want her around. You changed your face to look like her," Trish said "and then you hexed the house, knowing that we or one of us would run to Lilly for help with this because we didn't know anything about this stuff," Trish said. "How did you get us to the house?" she asked.

"Easy. We knew Sammy's parents died in a car crash, and we knew Ivy would use that road as a short cut, but just to make sure, I added something to the bottle of wine to make sure it went that way," Sarah said. "You see, I was there the whole time, so I knew I could freak out about the roads, and get scared," she said. "Then, all we needed was a weather spell, but that wasn't hard, considering its winter," she said. "Anyway, once we were in the house, Lilly started texting Natasha, because we knew she would have her phone," Sarah said laughing at me directly.

"You know what? You are evil," I stood up and said. "Did you gain anything from this? What profit did you make?" I snapped.

"Sit," Ivy ordered. "We do not need that nurse back in here."

"Actually, I think I need break from this," I said. "I am going to go get some coffee," I said and walked out.

"Natasha, come on, we need to know, however gruesome the details may be," Trish said as she followed me out. "Let's get the coffee, and go back in," she urged.

"Ok," I said. "Excuse me nurse. May we get a pot of coffee please?" I asked very politely.

"Yes. One moment, I will be back with it," she said.

"Thank you," I said as she turned and walked away. "Trish, I am so confused," I said as a tear fell from my eye.

"I know, but it will be ok. I am here, and I always will be," she said. "Don't hold Seth responsible. Talk to him later, and listen. Please" she begged.

"Here you go miss," the nurse said handing me the pot, and some foam cups.

"Thank you," I said and looked at the room.

"Come on, let's get this over with," Trish said as we walked back into the room.

"Good, they're back," Sarah said. "Now, shall we continue?" she asked. "Well, once we started texting, and scaring you guys, it was easy. I got absorbed by the curse, which was part of the plan, then Trish did, and that left you and Ivy, the two dramatic party girls, to do it all alone. And poor Natasha, afraid she would never see her family again," she laughed. "The only thing that we didn't plan for was how powerful the curse was. Lilly had no idea that even half of that could happen. But we improvised," she said so proud of their accomplishments.

"Ok, so then what happened?" Sammy asked still very confused.

"Easy. Natasha and Lilly saved the day and rescued us all. That's when the real fun started," she said. You see once we were all safe and out of harm's way, I put the revenge plan in motion, and that is when I tried to switch your lives. Then

Natasha and Lilly save the day again. Then the betrayal of Sammy and Seth came out, and Natasha's perfect little life was shattered. Then Trish pushes me down the stairs, killing my baby and then, well then, the plan came apart, because I was in the hospital as you see clearly and Sammy comes out of hiding unexpectedly," she said disgusted. "You see, we got nothing from this, because once I was pregnant, and Sammy comes to life, our plan was over. Lilly went on the run, and I am stuck here," she said.

I closed my eyes, and snapped my fingers. *'Lilly'*, I said and Lilly appeared. "Hi, Lilly, nice to see you again," I said glaring at her. "I have one question for you. Did we even break the curse?" I asked.

"Actually, no. It is still tact and will always be. But we got you out of there," she said fishing for sympathy.

"Well, in that case, LILLY to the House," I shouted and snapped my fingers. She disappeared.

"How….. No, bring her back," Sarah cried.

"Was that not part of your plan?" I asked. "So sorry to disappoint you," I snapped. "Bind their powers," I said and snapped my finders. "Now maybe neither of you can hurt anyone ever again. At least not with magic," I said.

"Please, I am begging you, don't take my best friend from me," Sarah cried.

"You can finish telling us how your plan was supposed to end," I said.

"Ok. Well it was supposed to end by sending you back to the day you were born, and switching you back, and then once you realized how your life you would be, you would undo it, and then things would be back to the way they are, and Ivy would pay off Sammy, in order to keep her mouth shut, and then Lilly and I would split the money, and leave," Sarah said.

"So all that for nothing," I said. "Wow, you two really did underestimate the power of friendship. We won't be broken," I said. "I really want to send you to the house, but maybe a mortal life alone, in prison, might be better," I said laughing. "Girls, what do you think? Any suggestions?" I asked.

"Send her to a mental institution," Sammy said laughing. "She would fit right in with all the other crazies."

"How about you send her back in time, when they would burn witches at the stake," Ivy said. "Let her try and make a profit off that."

"How about sending her to the book The Scarlet Letter?" Trish said, "She can forever bare the scar," Trish said laughing.

"How about we just let her be to live like a mortal and work like an honest man. Or, she can try to scam, but probably won't be any good at it, without her master mind by her side," I said. "She can spend her days, knowing what she has done. After all she has no powers, and obviously can't do anything without Lilly," I said smiling.

"Yeah, let's all go home, and leave her," Ivy said smiling.

"Yeah, come on girls, let go fix the mess she made for Natasha," Sammy said.

"Yeah, come on Natasha. Let's go home, and put the pieces back together," Trish said grabbing my hand.

"Ok, let's go home," I said as we all got up and walked away. Thank you guys so much, "I couldn't have gotten through that without you," I said.

"As we drove home, we were all relaxed and at peace. Our night mare had ended. Now all we had to do was fix the mess that had been made of our lives. Hey guys, can I write a book about this weekend?" I asked.

"You should. Just make sure it's fiction. No one would ever believe this could actually happen," Sammy said.

"How awesome would that be? The next bestseller is about this weekend," Trish said.

"We are home, guys," Ivy said. "Now Natasha, talk to Seth."

"I am going to," I said as we got out and walked into the house. The kids were sound asleep on the floor, and Seth and Scott, were sitting at the table, each drinking a beer. They turned and looked shocked by our smiles. "We're home," I said.

"Is everything ok?" Seth asked as he stood up.

"Yeah, can we talk," I asked as I hugged him. He really was the love of my life.

"I was hoping you would say that," he said hugging me.

"Guys, let's all go to the study. There's wine, and liquor," I said laughing.

"Please no more tequila," Ivy said laughing. "I don't think I will ever drink that again."

"Me either," I said. We all walked to the study. We all had so much to say.

"Here's to the future," Sammy said toasting her glass of wine.

"Yes, to the future," we said and drank.

"So Seth, Natasha has her next bestseller. She is going to write another book, about this weekend, but it's going to be in the fiction section. No one would believe it was real," Trish said.

"I can't wait to read it," Seth said smiling. Hopefully it can answer some questions we have about this weekend, he said laughing.

EPILOGUE

As the weeks turned to months, we still thought about that weekend, but only as a laugh. Trish got married-it was a beautiful event she wore a princess style white gown, and we were her bridesmaids. Her husband is truly a great guy, he takes wonderful care of her and the kids, and she is making a great career out of her photography.

Sammy is still doing the same, she is working her butt off, but it is paying off. She is the number one publicist in the business; she turned her marketing into a new career. She is also getting married next June.

Ivy is still herself. She and Logan went through a nasty divorce. Apparently our nightmare opened her eyes to herself, and she decided to make some changes, and he was one of them. He tried to take her to the cleaners, but she caught him with their maid, so he got nothing. She is doing well. She is opening her own women's shelter.

I wrote the book, and sure enough it was a bestseller. I ran into Sarah once, she looked rough. Her new life wasn't what she thought it would be, and occasionally I dreamt of Lilly in the house, spinning in circles, as it turned to waters of raging power, and winds of enormous strength, never knowing what was going to happen next. I hated the thought of putting someone through the hell we went through, but I find it ironic that she put us there, and her fate lies in the curse its self. I would really like to feel bad for her, but she has brought so much misfortune and misery to people, I can't feel bad.

Seth and I made up, and it is all in the past. He now comes with me on more events, and is no longer in the shadows. He is even working on the cover of my next book; it is wonderful to have him by my side, instead of behind me. Although I am still angry with him for having an affair, I know it wasn't really his fault. He was under a spell, and I choose to believe that is why. I know it will take time, but I am willing to do the time.

About a week ago, we heard the news that the house had caught fire, and burned to the ground, we chuckled to our selves, knowing no one would ever live the hell we did. It is so strange to think that evil actually lives in our world, and people really do practice magic, and have magic. Most people think it is just fantasy, but we know the truth. Ivy, Sammy, Trish and I still talk and get together once a month but we stay modern; no curses, and definitely no tequila, well at least not without proper supervision.

Other Books by D.C. Cole

Trust Only No One

This novel is about a woman, Lady Victoria, who is married to Lord Dominic; one is evil, abusive, and causes her to fear for her life and the life of her niece. Her best friend Natasha helps her escape and finds out that they are sisters and actually very wealthy. They were in an orphanage together as children and raised very poor, which is why Victoria married Dominic. There are many surprises throughout the book that leads to a very exciting ending and the beginning into the sequel. **ISBN: 978-1886528020**

Mommy What are All those Lights for on the Bus?

D.C. Cole is an author from ASA Publishing Company in Historic Downtown Monroe, Michigan, with her children book titled, "Mommy What are All those Lights for on the bus?" Her children book aims toward the educational field of providing illustrated information to identify the lights that are used on a

school bus, as well as the meaning of those lights, including how to safely get on the bus. **ISBN: 978-0982813546**

Truth or Lie

This book is about teaching children the differences between telling a lie and telling the truth. Most parents struggle with this lesson because kids don't understand what telling a lie means. **ISBN: 978-1886528048**

Enjoy the fascinating educational children books with your family, and relax in the evening with your choice of selected mystery novels by this wonderful and gifted author, D.C. Cole.